A Time Before the End

A Time
Before the End

A Novel

Gilmer White

A Time Before the End is a work of fiction.

Copyright ©2011 Gilmer White
ISBN 978-0-578-09490-8
All rights reserved under
International and Pan-American Copyright

Published by Low Country Press
Savannah, Georgia
www.lowcountrypress.net

Library of Congress Cataloging-in-Publication Data
is available on request.

Manufactured in the United States of America

First Edition: October 2011
9 8 7 6 5 4 3 2 1

DEDICATION

This book is dedicated to JoAnn and Jason.

ACKNOWLEDGEMENTS

Gratitude goes to Barbara Dunn,
whose editorial skills and clear advice
kept me on track when I needed them most.
Thanks also to Jim Dunn, a good friend
who has mastered the art of listening.

Special appreciation goes to all
who lent me their presence during those
"dark night of the soul" times
when I was wrestling with some
of the mythological themes
that seem to be an integral part
of the fabric of life itself
and have no end.
A TIME BEFORE THE END
could not have been written without you.
You all know who you are!

GW

There is an appointed time for everything,
and there is a time for every event under heaven.

Ecclesiastes 3:1
New American Standard Bible

"Be calm don't cry," answered the frog,
"I can surely be of assistance.
But what will you give me if I fetch your toy for you."

Grimm's Fairy Tales, No. 1, "The Frog King"

PROLOGUE

Hanover, North Carolina 1930

The cold, northeast wind whipped across the lake throwing its force against the worn-out, wooden pier standing in its path. It stood there, unflinching, like an over-the-hill boxer, taking the punches head-on, its slime-covered pilings and cross-timbers shaking and groaning but refusing to give in to the pounding. The woman standing at its entrance holding the hands of the two boys did not seem to mind the turmoil surrounding her. Her grandfather had built this pier more than fifty years before, and during its lifetime it had withstood everything nature could throw at it including a few hurricanes, so a northeast blow was nothing new.

"I can't believe they're taking her down," she whispered into the wind. Accepting the enormity of the impending event was what had brought her out in the approaching storm. This would be the last chance for Rebecca Porter to see the pier and honor the memory of her grandfather before the workers came tomorrow to tear it down.

She was a shapely, pretty woman of thirty with high cheekbones and deeply recessed, indigo-blue eyes partly obscured by the ridge of her brow. Her tousled, strawberry blond hair swirled with the wind around her face.

"Come on boys," Becky said, pushing forward against the wind onto the trembling pier, pulling each by the hand.

"Momma," young Ben Porter said, "I'm scared. Let's go back."

He was a small, fair, delicate looking boy of twelve with a poised, almost feminine step. Like a stubborn mule, he tried to counter her motion by firmly planting his feet on the pier.

"You're always scared, Ben," the older boy said. "Come on, Aunt Becky, let's go."

Luther Quinn had just turned fifteen and was her sister, Lenore's son. She hadn't wanted to bring him because she had meant the event for Ben and herself, but Lenore had used that unsteady, breathless voice that told Becky she and her husband Cyrus were at it again, so Becky had picked up Luther on her way to the lake. He was like a giant next to Ben. Already over six feet, his lean muscular body was topped by an unusually long, craning neck. Balanced on top was a perfectly round head that looked as if it had been halved and put back together slightly off center, giving his face a lopsided look.

Becky led the boys halfway down the pier to a small wooden bench that faced the water.

"Let's sit here for a moment," she said, drawing the boys down beside her.

Pushing her hand deep into the pocket of her pea-coast, she found what she was seeking, withdrawing it with her fist clenched. Like a blossom slowly unfolding, she opened her hand.

Resting in her palm was a small gold brooch encrusted with clusters of diamonds, emeralds, and rubies. She held it with her hands cupped, as if she were holding a small bird she was afraid of squeezing too tight. Becky extended her hands to let the boys peek inside. The stared at the brooch for a moment, and then looked up at her. What was so special about an old piece of jewelry anyway, and what made her hold it like it was something alive?

Becky pushed her trembling hands closer to the boys.

"Ben, your great-grandfather who built this pier left the brooch for me in his will. Not to my momma and daddy, but to me. I guess he knew how much I loved him. And that's really why we're here—to honor Granddaddy."

Samuel Berry was a sea captain in the last days of the giant sailing ships. He was a huge man of ample girth, weighing almost 300 pounds and renowned for his feats of strength and gusto with a knife and fork at the kitchen table. After he retired from the sea, he opened a small boatyard and later contracted with the City to build the pier. It was apparent from the beginning that Becky would be his favorite grandchild. Whenever the old sailor arrived for Sunday dinner at his daughter's table, Becky would climb over his stout legs onto his lap, and he would tell her takes of his stirring adventures on the high seas. As Becky grew older, she would listen to him patiently as he repeated the same stories with preposterous exaggerations, and would smile with wry amusement at an old man entertaining himself with his own creations. And hadn't that been what he was doing all along?

One wind blown autumn day when she was sixteen, something happened to make Becky Porter change her mind. Samuel, using a cane, came to her in the garden late one afternoon. She knew he was failing fast now, and moved quickly to meet him. In one hand he carried a small wooden box.

"Darlin'," he said. He liked to call her that. "Do ye remember me story about being shipwrecked?"

"Yes, Granddaddy," she said.

It had been one of his tallest tales. Shipwrecked on an uninhabited island in the South Pacific for six months, the only survivor of a vicious storm at sea, blown ashore clinging to a mast, living off of berries, fish and coconuts.

"Did I ever tell ye about the other ship that was blown onto the rocks and smashed to pieces. A horrible sight, it was."

13

"No, Granddaddy."

"Well, it happened. A Russ ship it were. I found its colors when they were blown ashore. I found something else too. This box. Saw it the next day floating in the surf and waded out to get it."

It was a small box, worn by time and its exposure to the sea. He opened the lid and extended it to her. Inside was the brooch encrusted with jewels that she now held nestled in her palm. It rested on a piece of stained script that was obviously Russian.

"Had the writing translated, I did. Said it had been fashioned for something called a soiree at court during the reign of Peter the Great. Been in me sea chest ever since."

Becky took the brooch into her hand and turned it toward the fading light. As the light caught it, the diamonds came alive with a flashing blue tint. The emeralds and rubies were interspersed with diamonds so that their colors glowed from the iridescence.

"Its beyond beautiful," she said.

"It be yours," he replied.

Becky continued to stare at the brooch resting in the center of her cupped hands. Like a swinging pendulum, the dazzling kaleidoscope of colors thrown off by the glittering gems had brought her to an almost hypnotic state. Suddenly, all of her senses came alive as she realized Luther was standing over her. As she looked up, she saw him trembling, a distant, fixed look in his eyes.

"Aunt Becky, I hear voices," he said.

"Luther, it's just the wind howling," she said.

"No, I hear them talking," he said.

Becky realized what was happening. Luther had recently started complaining about hearing sounds, which he described as voices. Becky knew what was going on in her sister's household. At first the *voices* had been discounted as attempts by Luther to gain attention. When the voices didn't stop, a psychologist called them an internalized dialogue—Luther had developed a fantasy life. But something was different this time. Becky had never seen him like this before. He was extremely agitated. His face had turned red with pent up emotion. She was frightened as she rose to face him.

She placed one of his hands on his arm.

"Calm down, Luther," she said.

"No," he said. "Don't say that to me."

As the words came from his mouth, Luther brought his hand down sharply on Becky's other hand—the one holding the brooch.

Becky Porter's horror stricken cry was transformed by the wind into the howl of a wounded animal. She fell to her knees, her mouth open, gasping, trying to suck air into her hyperventilating lungs. Her hands flailed at the pier's planking beneath her, hoping to grasp the brooch before it fell in the swirling water under the pier. All she felt was the wood and the wide cracks between the planks. The heirloom brooch with its weight of precious jewels was gone, lost in the waters beneath. She began to scream again. Ben knelt beside her and picked up her cry, his small mouth contorted. Luther stood silently looking down at them, his face still red. As Becky knelt, sobbing, she was startled by the grasp of a hand on her shoulder. She rose on her knees to find what appeared to be an apparition staring at her. This time, she screamed louder.

The living being standing before Becky Porter had the hard, worn look of hunger on its face and exhaustion in its hollow, unblinking eyes. Stiff, unruly, dirty black hair framed a face dominated by a wide full mouth and large, caked, cracked lips. Its caramel colored skin was soiled by the marks of harsh physical activity. Rag doll clothes covered its body. At the far extension of its reach hung a dirty, shabbily dressed creature of seven or eight.

At the sight of the surreal beings that Becky now realized were a woman and a child, Becky began to lose whatever composure she had remaining.

"What's happened, lady?" the woman asked Becky Porter, her voice thick with the rhythm of Negro spirituals and African intonations.

"Oh my God," Becky cried hysterically. "My brooch just

fell in the water, and they're tearing the pier down tomorrow. I'll never find it then. Oh my God!"

"It valuable, mum?" the haggard woman asked.

Becky was still sucking wind, trying to catch her breath.

"Woman, it's worth a fortune," she said.

The wind had settled down around them. The imposing stranger's unblinking eyes had opened wide as if she were looking into Becky's soul. Her next words were spoken like a command.

"You do something for me," the woman said. "I ask you for a favor. You do it, I find your brooch."

"We don't have time to talk about favors," Becky said. "If you're going to do it, you've got to act now."

The woman laid her soiled, chapped hands on Becky's shoulders. Her eyes held Becky's in a long embrace.

"Lady, lady, this is something you *must* do."

Becky looked at the weathered planking at her feet. Her shoulders slumped.

"What is it you want," she whispered. "Tell me, please."

"When I find the brooch, I'll tell you. You must trust me."

Becky looked directly into the woman's eyes. They looked like the obsidian stone she had seen at a museum display. They were unyielding.

Becky slowly nodded her agreement.

"Lady, I need you to hold my girl Olive's hand while I find it," the woman said.

Becky gingerly took the dirty black girl's hand in hers. Like the woman, she was dressed in soiled, shabby clothes. Olive looked up at Becky with the sharp pain of fatigue and hunger in her dark eyes. Ben dressed in corduroy pants and warm matching jacket, looked at Olive with wide-eyed amazement. Luther turned away to look at the water. To a stranger, standing nearby in that part of North Carolina in the autumn of 1930, it seemed a most incongruous scene: a pretty white woman with tears in her eyes, holding the hand of a dirty, black girl in a sack dress who timidly reached out to a slender, neatly dressed white boy, who took her hand in his own.

The woman was Charlene Delome, a name given her by her

French father and African mother, but she called herself Carly to honor the broken pronunciation of the illiterate slaves who worked on the plantation in Haiti.

Carly didn't want her tattered clothes capturing air so she reached down and pulled the back hem of the dress between her legs and tied the end to the rope around her waist.

"Show me where it fell," she said.

Becky pointed to a spot beyond the bench near the railing.

Carly sat on the edge of the pier for a moment then lowered herself into the murky water below. The cold shock of the water tore through her exposed flesh. Above Becky's sobs sounded like the lonesome wail of a train in the night. Taking a deep breath, Carly slid beneath the surface. When she reached the bottom and extended her hands, they quickly became entangled in the undulating, eel-like, aquatic grass that covered the bottom. As her fingers painstakingly worked their way through the sinuously moving grass, fatigue began to drain her energy. Frantically, she began to tear at the slimy, tentacles opposing her. As the last of her oxygen was used and the remaining breath forced from her lungs, she felt the presence of the Loa, the Voodoo spirits of her native country Haiti. In her failing consciousness, they were speaking with her— giving her a sign. As blackness began to close in, she pushed her hand beneath the lake grass one more time, and there her fingers closed around an object.

Carly emerged from the lake like a creature from the deep, water cascading from her body, gasping for air, her black hair twisted into licorice stick shapes that covered her face. She was shivering uncontrollably and holding the many-jeweled brooch like a supplicant making an offering. A frigid smile broke onto her face.

PART ONE

A TIME TO BEGIN

THE PROPHECY

Carly Delome sits in the kitchen of Becky Porter's home facing an ancient, pot-bellied, iron stove, which has been stoked and now is beginning to display a red glow. Her straight, black hair has been combed and brushed and lies level with her shoulders. She wears an old gown of Becky's and sips on a cup of hot cider. Her face changes countenance as she rocks in and out of the shadows cast by the evening's pall. The signs of youth and age come and go. Becky Porter sits nearby, studying the features of the woman who would risk her life to find a brooch. Becky waits for the woman to speak, but the only sound she hears is the soft humming of a plaintive lullaby.

"Tell me what I need to know to help you," Becky finally asks.

Carly turns to look at Becky, her generous lips parted to speak. When the words come, her speech has changed since she spoke at the pier. Each word now stands out as if surrounded by air—each word articulated with confidence, a hint of French accent on her tongue.

"Olive and I came here from our Haitian colony in Miami to look for her father who last wrote from here. She and I are not related, but it was the wish of her dying mother, and I am honor bound to try to find him."

"Is that all? You just want me to help you find her father?"

"No, not all. We have no money left. It is the times. We live in a tent camp down by the lake. Everyone is hungry. There is little work . . . only hard labor for a few. Mostly we beg and share what we get. It is so hard on the girl Olive. We need food and a warm place to stay until we move on. This is my wish for finding your brooch."

Becky cups her chin in her hand. She only has to think for a moment. Sure, she can do it. The sheriff's office! He can easily find out the girl's father is still in these parts. As for a place to stay . . .

Her thoughts are disturbed by the presence of Luther in the doorway. Behind him stands a tall woman with pale skin and flowing auburn hair.

"Hi sis. Came to pick up Luther and heard part of what happened."

Becky rises and kisses Lenore Quinn on the cheek. She smiles inwardly. Her sister always wants a blow-by-blow account of the latest news and gossip from around town. Listening is like a catharsis from the turmoil of her present life. Becky always gives her what she needs.

"Okay," she says. "Here's the whole story."

While they talk, Luther Quinn edges closer to Carly. He cranes his long neck and peers into her face. When Carly returns his look, it is as if she is seeing him for the first time. The head, like a circus ball balanced on a long flexible pole. Oh, she thought, look at the cleft in his face, and the color of his skin. It was like a bruise changing from black to purple to a lighter shade not quite on the chart. She had seen these things before.

As Becky and Lenore step into the hall, Luther starts to move in a circle around Carly, inspecting her, tentatively extending his fingers toward her, but withdrawing them quickly as if he has touched a hot stove. When he completes the circle, he is facing Carly again. He raises his hands to cover his ears. He begins to shake.

Carly has not moved.

"What is happening to you, Luther?" she asks.

"I'm hearing the voices again. They want me to do something. I'm scared."

As if controlled by a rheostat, the light surrounding Luther seems to fade. Despite the heat from the stove, Carly begins to shiver. Seeping through the very pores of the house, an amorphous presence invades the room, curling its way around Carly's feet as if it were an old cat, stroking her arms with the touch of a feather, letting its weight be felt in her lap. These are things Carly has experienced before. The dark Petro spirits of the Voodoo religion—the black magic, evil spirits—have entered the room and surrounded her. The Rada, the sweet Loa spirits, have been forced into the background. Luther, a look of terror on his face, backs out of the room, his eyes still on Carly.

The shadows of the evening move through the windowpane into the room. Carly's dark eyes look but do not see. She begins to rock. The cadence of her rocking picks up pace. Faster and faster she moves, the rocker almost tipping over as she reaches the apex of her movement. Suddenly, she throws her head back and begins to shake. She is crying and speaking in a strange tongue. Her back arches and then bends forward as if a heavy weight has been placed on it.

Slowly, slowly, the rocking begins to decelerate and finally stops. The trance that has possessed her is over. She is exhausted.

Carly raises her head to find Becky holding her.

"God, what is it?" Becky cries. "Are you okay?"

Carly looks into the depth of Becky's indigo blue eyes.

"Yes, I'm okay, but something frightening has happened that I must tell you about."

Who is this woman from the pier who speaks in tongues and exhibits different personalities? Becky's hand goes to her mouth. Her eyes open wide. Her voice trembles.

"Ooookay," Becky says. "Tell me, please."

"First, I must tell you about me. I was born in Haiti on a

plantation to an African slave. The slaves believe in the power of Voodoo. I am a healer and spirit person they call Mambo. What my people do not have from medicine or the church, I give them in another way.

"Here is what I was told while in the trance by the Rada, the good spirits, when my mind was not my own. The evil spirits, the Petro, the ones I have cast out of many tortured souls, have followed me here. They seek revenge, but my faith is too strong for them. When they found the boy Luther on the pier, they sensed his weakness and entered him. He has brought them into your house, and they are legion. I do not have enough power to cast them all out. The Rada spirits say the Petro will try to destroy everyone in this house. They say there will be madness, murder, and mayhem. Finally, a savior will appear. They say it will all come to pass *at a time before the end.*"

BEN
AFTER THE WAR

He looked in the mirror and for a moment didn't see him self. Didn't feel anything either. Blank. Just looked in the mirror so he wouldn't have to look back at the woman. When he finally focused on himself, standing before him was a young man of medium height with the delicate features of a slightly built ballet dancer. Blond hair and blue eyes stood out against a deep tan, but you could see how fair skinned he was by the white area his bathing suit had covered.

A sudden gust of wind from off the ocean snapped the shade drawn over the open window in the motel room and brought his attention back to what lay to his rear. Ben Porter pulled on his jeans, turned slowly, and walked to the foot of the bed, his steps as polished and precise as the dancer he resembled. The woman was looking at him, solemn lines of concern drawn around oval, emerald green eyes. Disheveled, light brown hair clung to her damp forehead. A rumpled sheet was pulled around her so that her nipples were covered, but the rest of her breasts were exposed.

"Look, Sarah . . . I'm sorry," he said.

A wry, pained expression tugged at the corner of Sarah's mouth.

A Time Before the End

"You know how I feel about you, Ben. It's hard on me too. It's always the same thing, isn't it?" she said.

"Yeah . . . that's what they keep saying, but I don't know. The dreams scare the hell out of me, but there's something else wrong. You know it . . . "

"I keep hearing you in the night. That's all I know . . . and what happens afterwards."

The thought of the dreams stuck with him. That's what the psychiatrists at the Veteran's Hospital in Raleigh wanted to talk about—the dreams and the nightmares they spawned. That's why he'd made the 300-mile roundtrip for the past three years . . .

In the barren, wasteland of his dreams, everything is white and sterile. He is on a journey from home to a place he has visited often. When he gets ready to return, nothing is familiar anymore. He tries to find his way back home but only runs into dead ends. He asks directions, but all he gets are stares from hollow eyes. Every night is a different story, but the ending is always the same. He is irretrievably lost. He is terrified.

Ben could hear the soft sound of Sarah breathing. The room had never been so quiet. Outside, the sea and the wind had fallen still. As Ben stood facing her, Sarah rose from the bed and reached for her robe. Her graceful movements revealed a slightly arched back and firm buttocks; and, as she turned to close her robe, her pubic area and large rounded breasts. Sarah Hardy was really something to look at.

Ben Porter came home from the war a hero. A graduate of the only all-white high school in Hanover, it seemed everyone knew Ben with his quick smile and easy ways. And hadn't he looked great in his uniform when he came home for the first time? There were newspaper articles about his capture in the war and how he planned an escape from a Stalag using himself as a decoy so that the more vulnerable of the flight crews who were being starved and tortured could go ahead. Of course, there was the story concerning his confinement at Walter Reed and then the brief mention that he had enrolled at the University of North Carolina in Chapel Hill. It all added up to instant fame until the stories about him started to spread around town—the stories about his relationship with a Negro woman before the war and a half-white child who lived with her across the tracks. Then the gossip that he was being treated as an outpatient at the VA hospital for something ungodly the Nazi's did to him added even more fuel to the fire.

After completing medical treatment, Ben finally came home for good. The Sea Oats was an old motel, beaten by the weather and raked by hurricanes. Ben took over as manager mainly as a favor for family friends who couldn't keep a sober innkeeper at the isolated row of cabins spread out near the inlet like washed up sea-shells. The job was supposed to be for only a few short months until they found someone else, but it turned out differently.

After the hospital, and his mother Becky's forebodings, and the furtive glances and whispers, he found a sense of peace in the isolation of the old motel. Ben became the live-in innkeeper, care-taker, and maid, in a one-person operation catering to fishermen and the occasional tourists attracted by its "castaway's" mystique. When business was slow, which was most of the time, he would read from an armful of books brought in from the library, or pull out his beat-up Royal typewriter and write about life as he had never known it until he went off to the war.

Sometimes, he would put out the NO VACANCY sign and drive up the single roadway lying between the ocean and the Cape Fear River to a pavilion where bathers gathered to swim and eat. It was his only way now of getting beyond himself and feeling con-nected to the outside world. It was a kind of outer presence that often almost moved him to tears. He could feel the beauty surround-ing him in little things like the soft, almost invisible hair on the arms of female sunbathers as they passed by, or in the movement of lips as they formed a smile, or in eyes that told their story apart from the face in which they were fixed. When he couldn't stand the beauty anymore, he drove back to the motel and tried to write about it.

The pavilion was where he met Sarah standing at the hot

dog stand in her bathing suit. He wouldn't call her beautiful, but she was pretty with a nice figure and a kind of feminine animation like that pantomimed by mimes or by actresses in silent movies. He was staring at the piano-like movement of her fingers as she tried to balance six hotdogs. When she became aware of his presence and turned to face him, a momentary, polite smile crossed her lips.

"They're for my friends," she said.

Ben smiled back.

"What about the drinks?" he said.

She motioned with her head.

"Oh, we're sitting at the table over there. I'm coming back for the drinks."

"I'll carry them for you," he said.

That was the way they met, a nice-looking, spirited girl with sand on her legs and a handsome, young man with the flowing moves of a dancer.

Her friends knew Sarah Hardy as a "beach person," which was something like the connection between the term "Conch" and someone born in Key West. She and her family had lived at Carolina Beach for what seemed forever, but when they moved back to town to avoid the worsening hurricane seasons, Sarah stayed behind. She rented an apartment and worked as a waitress at Pauline's, an up-scale seafood and steak restaurant near the pavilion. With her grace and skill as a waitress and knowledge of wines, she was a favorite with the patrons. A wink from her to anyone who sat at her table said: "I know exactly how you want to be treated and the service you expect, and I'll take care of you." Outside of her close circle of girl friends, she had a reputation for being aloof—some even called her haughty—but those who knew her best attributed Sarah's demeanor to something else—boundaries formed as a result of a traumatic incident when she was much younger. If anyone knew what it was, they weren't saying, and her friends had learned to accept her as she was. She could surf with the best of the surfer boys, and was constantly but politely rebuffing their crude approaches, which had the effect of bringing them back just in case she changed her mind. But it was a rare event for Sarah to be seen in the company of any male, which got people talking; but if she knew about the rumors, she never let on. She was the very attractive woman who no one could figure out, an enigma really, but one who year after year remained the same.

That's why it shocked everyone when Sarah took up with Ben Porter. It shocked Ben, too, because her reputation had preceded her, as had his. The guys smirked and her girlfriends smiled when Ben started hanging out at the beach, clearly positioning himself where he might have a chance to talk with her. One slow evening at the pavilion near the end of summer, Ben saw her sitting alone in the bar. He slipped down from his stool and walked over to her, smiled, and asked her to go out with him. She gave him a smile back that told of a decision already made. No one could understand it! A good looking woman like Sarah Hardy who could have had her pick from the field, choosing instead a guy like him.

Ben and Sarah's favorite pastime was to walk on the beach and talk about what had happened in their lives that day. They held hands and waded in the shallow water where the waves ran up on the shore. Sometimes, they fished in the surf, and cooked the catch in her apartment and ate to candlelight and drank the chilled white wine she had selected. On one particular night that stuck in their memories, they danced at the pavilion to the frenzied, eclectic beat of one of the local bands. The sensuous motion of their bodies drew a crowd who surrounded them and yelled their approval. Then the music ended in a crashing crescendo and Ben and Sarah stood bent over facing each other with a wild look of breathlessness, trying to laugh, with hope in their eyes, as if to say, "Wow, something's going on here. Let's just let it happen."

On an autumn evening when the first hint of nor'easters and hurricanes were in the air, Sarah turned to Ben and took his arm in hers.

"We can't go on not knowing. We need to tell each other about ourselves if we are ever to have something together. Don't you think?"

Ben nodded, and turned to face her. She put her finger to his lips.

"Please, let me go first," she said. "I had this thing—a relationship with a soldier I met at the USO. My girlfriends and I were all underage, but somehow I got in. He was just a boy, not much older than I was. His name was Jake, and we thought we had something special, but I was young and didn't know what life was about back then. We just acted it out and then I found out he had been killed in the battle of the Bulge, and I was pregnant. I didn't know how to deal with it, and felt I couldn't go to my parents. They sent you away back then. Then I did something that has haunted me ever since. And this is where I am today. I don't know anything about relationships."

Ben put his fist to his mouth. His anguished sobs sounded as if they were being torn from his throat. He hurt so much for Sarah and had held his own pain inside too long. When he composed himself, he told her all that had happened to him in the war and afterward when he was captured. He told her about his life since, the dreams and nightmares, and his visits to the VA, and what they said was wrong with him. She was looking at his face, intent on every word. Then he told her something else.

"I have a child who is part Negro. It happened before I went off to war, when I was young and in training. I didn't know anything about relationships back then either. Her name is Rachel. She's almost thirteen now. I usually get her every other weekend—sometimes every weekend if her mother has to work. I didn't know how to deal with it in public at first . . . I mean her color, but she was so young and innocent and I was so screwed up, I decided it didn't make any difference. I know I should have told you sooner."

Sarah took Ben's spastic, clenching fist into her hands.

"Ben, it's OK. I've known all along. You can't keep something like that secret around here. It made you special to me. Look, here we are with all our secrets out in the open . . . nothing left to hide. What's that going to mean for each of us? You and me? Rachel?"

Ben freed his hand and turned Sarah to face him.

"I guess we need to find out," he said.

They crossed the sand dunes hand in hand and headed for Ben's car.

LUTHER'S GAMBIT

It was a bleak afternoon in the early summer of 1955. Dark, low-hanging, rain clouds were rapidly moving in from the east, and the imminent, oxygen-fresh smell of lightning was in the air. He stood unmoving, squinting, looking somewhere beyond the rectangular, razor sharp, barbed-wire fence that enclosed the dusty prison yard. After so many years in the State Penitentiary just outside of Raleigh, North Carolina, it had become an engrained ritual, his eyes peering into the distance, searching, as if seeking something hidden he had missed before.

By any standard, Luther Quinn was a huge man. Standing six-feet, nine-inches tall and weighing about 350 pounds, Luther was solid muscle, a result of years of hard labor on the chain and road gangs. When he looked directly at people, his face appeared to have been struck solidly enough by a sledgehammer to knock it lopsided, giving it the appearance of an object viewed thru a prism, the left side several millimeters below the right. Prison fights and the resulting scars that marked both sides of his face and long neck had earned him the reputation of having a hair trigger and nasty temper that prompted unpredictable, violent actions. No one, not

33

even the most crazed bullies among the prison population wanted to tangle with him.

As he continued to linger, Luther's thoughts and fixation on the distance were interrupted by raucous shouts and peels of laughter to his rear. One thing he didn't like was to be disturbed when he was remembering things. Luther swung around to face the noise. When he saw the diminutive, dunce-like figure cowering before the taunts of a group of shirtless, muscle-bound inmates, be broke into a crooked smile.

Luther's singular passion all these long years inside was to get outside: to be free again, to see his Momma and to get revenge. Unfortunately, all his schemes to break out had failed to work, but now . . . now, in the blink of an eye, as he stared at the wee creature before him, new visions of a plan to escape danced before his eyes. Luther knew that the little man standing there, a spanking-new inmate, had rare abilities that could be put to use.

The problem was that standing in his way were a hulking group of jeering, mocking, prison bullies closing in on the small gnome-like person like vultures circling a wounded animal.

Luther moved to the back of the pack and peered in at the diminutive figure. Cutting a swath through the mob before him, he moved forward until he stood facing the trembling, little man.

"He's mine, boys," he said. He looked down at the startled figure staring up at him. "Hello, Pender," he said. "What the hell are you doing here?"

"Is that you, Lu . . . Luther?" said the strange looking creature standing before him. "Is it really you?"

Pender Hicks had been called a lot of names—dwarf, runt, cull—to name a few, all designed to mock his four-feet, two-inch-height, but the moniker that finally stuck was "Ape." And it was easy to see why. He had an abnormal amount of hair covering his torso and legs, and long hairy arms that almost touched the ground and swung like pendulums as he walked. Adding to these distracting features were a sloping forehead and bushy eyebrows. When he was prodded to mimic an ape, the resemblance was uncanny. His saving grace was his eyes—large and crystal blue like a china doll's—and his lips, which were as plump and red as a juicy plum.

Pender knew Luther from a place called Dry Pond near the outskirts of Hanover, North Carolina.

"Thirty-three or Thirty-four it was, if I got my dates right," Pender later told an acquaintance. "Just knew it was after I run away from Pastor Brown's and joined the circus. Should'a left a lot earlier but that's another story. Anyway, they called it a circus because we had one old broken down elephant that could still do some tricks and a few halfway trained horses, but it was really a carnival because the main things people came to see was the side shows and the freaks. Anyway, we had to winter near Hanover at a place called Dry Pond. Because of the Depression, nobody had nothin' and that's about what we were workin' for—nothin'. Old Mr. Johnson, the owner, always put on a few shows for the locals to make ends meet, and that's where I met Luther—at one of them shows. It was real cold that day, I remember, and we hadn't even finished with our first group, and already I could hear the barker out front callin' in more people, mostly folks with hardly a cent to their name.

"'Come on in folks, see tha amazing freak show! See tha Snake Man. Deadly poisonous, straight from the wilds of Brazil! Watch the Rubber Man. See him bend like a pretzel! And folks, take a gander at the fattest lady south of the Mason Dixon. Try to guess her weight!'

"When I heard that, I looked down the row and she was sittin' on a bench made of iron or something to support her weight, wearin' a huge polka-dot dress that was as big as a tent. It's funny but I still remember her big red lips that looked like those they paint on dolls, and her sayin' to the guy tryin' to guess her weight, 'Come on honey, you know four-fifty ain't gonna git it.' I always liked her, and people laughed when they saw us together. And that's

35

the same way it went with the rest of us freaks. They just laughed at us. Finally all the people who came to the first performance was standin' in front of my cage and it was my turn.

"'See the African Ape Boy. Folks, you won't believe your eyes.'

"They had me all made up, my face like a boy's and my body like an ape's. I was swingin' from one rung to another, eatin' a banana and gruntin', and everyone was laughin'. I never said a single word until the very end, and that's when I dropped to the floor, ran at the crowd and shook the cage. 'Me Ape Boy,' I grunted real loud in a way that sounded like it might come from an ape. Everybody jumped back, except one. Luther stood there grinnin' and winkin'. Like I told him when we was closin' down for the evening: "Even a fool can tell it ain't real," I said, "but most folks who come to carnivals don't care. They come to see us freaks. They see what they want to see.

"In a way, it was weird," Pender said. "Him bein' so big with that long neck and strange lookin' face, and me bein' so small and lookin' the way I do; but it worked out, and we got to be buddies until they caught him and sent him away for those murders. I never seen him again after that. But yeah, we spent a lot of time together. He liked all the new tricks I was learning how to do . . . especially the escape tricks like getting' out of the ropes and the coffin, and he laughed when I showed him how easy it was if you was built the way I was."

The storm was closing in and puffs and swirls of dust from the dry prison yard were muddying the air when Luther led Pender from the yard to the prison block.

"I thought you might still be with the carnival," Luther said. "What the hell happened? How'd you end up here?"

"Jeez, Luther. I thought you had heard from your momma

or somebody. With all the hard times, the carnival folded before we could get further south to Alabama and Mississippi where we'd done real good before. Old Mr. Johnson—he's dead now—just called us all in one day and told us he couldn't keep goin' and he was forced to sell the carnival lock, stock, and barrel. I hung around there with some of the others livin' in one of the tents that hadn't been sold, but there was no way a bunch of freaks like us could make a livin' 'round there, so I hitched south to Florida and got on as a roust-a-bout with Barnum Bailey. Workin' for a real circus! I knew it was what I was meant to do . . . where I belonged. And I worked there all through the war and afterwards until I got hurt and couldn't work no more, and when I got well, they weren't hirin' and I didn't have no money left. Well, to make a long story short, I drifted back north lookin' for work or any other way to survive, and got caught stealin', and you know the rest . . . here I am."

"How long you in for Pender?" Luther asked.

"Five years. That's what they gave me."

"You won't last that long here, Pender. A little guy like you. Ain't no way you can survive. Ain't no way I can protect you all the time either. Those bulls back there will gang rape you in the shower or someplace else, and the guards will look the other way. When they get tired of you, some other cons will pick you up. If you ain't dead by then, you might as well be."

Luther took the little man by the arm and pulled him close. He stooped to speak into his ear. "I've got this idea, Pender," he whispered. "Your skills, you can break out of here. I know it. I seen you back at the carnival, remember? I'll help you set it up. Then I'll tell you how we both can escape."

Pender dropped his head.

"I . . . I don't know Luther. I only got five. I'll probably get paroled in two or three."

Luther squeezed Pender's arm until the small man groaned. "You ain't got no choice, Pender," he said. "I'm going to see my momma and then I'm going to get even with Ben for what he did to me."

THE STORM

The storm came up slowly, rolling in from the south, carrying a belly full of water sucked up by tornado-shaped ocean downspouts. The leading edge of the storm was a cruel, unrelenting wind that tore through Kure Beach, hammering the storefront signs, whipping sand from the dunes, and propelling hotdog wrappers, paper cups, and other loose beach trash across the deserted oceanfront road. When the storm momentarily stalled, it hovered low over the small community like a giant helicopter, its enormous rotor blades beating the surface below as if it were preparing to land. Then came the storm's angry punch to the gut. The black, distended, water-laden cloud split like an overripe melon. Rain burst forth from the breech in torrents covering the roads and sidewalks in sheets driven by the wind, making any kind of vision impossible. Some storm veterans stood in doorways with their arms wrapped around them to ward off the chill, and watched as the storm inched its way north.

Standing on the small rear porch of the Sea Oats Motel, looking south at the approaching storm, Sarah slowly shook her head and turned to face Ben.

"No way can I get out of it," she said. "I talked to Pauline, and she said a lot of regulars still have reservations, and there's the usual Saturday crowd at the oyster bar who'd be there in anything short of a full blown hurricane. On top of everything else, there's a convention in town and some of them are calling. It's going to fill up early. Pauline even had to bring James in to shuck, and you know how far he has to come. Upside is, I'll be tip-heavy when I get back. If the storm blows over, we'll plan something nice for tomorrow."

Rachel stood on the deck close by, her arms crossed for warmth, looking at the storm obliterating everything in its path from view.

Ben turned to look at the black clouds moving up the coast. He reached out and pulled Sarah close.

"If it doesn't stall, you'll be in good shape," he said. "If you can't hang loose at Pauline's, try to make it to the Pavilion. Camp out there until it blows over. But be sure to check in with me. This thing looks like it's going to be a mess."

They had been living together for six months off and on, really. Sarah kept her lease on the apartment but was spending more and more time at the motel helping Ben. Business had picked up because of the recommendations from Pauline's by way of Sarah and her friends, and Ben was able to afford a new neon sign with an arrow pointing down the road to the motel. Of course, it wasn't any Holiday Inn or some of the new, fancy motels that were breaking ground, but it was clean and comfortable, and Sarah saw to it that it stayed that way. Even Ben's trips to the VA had produced some positive results, and the great thing was that Rachel really took to Sarah. It was beginning to feel like a real family.

Rachel was seven when Ben finally came home to manage the motel. His behavior had hurt and angered Olive, Rachel's mother, when he had returned but had made no effort to see them. What about the past? What about the promises? What about the child they had brought into the world? People continued to talk about the white southern boy who dared to cross the line with his Negro girlfriend, and then had ditched her and their kid after he'd returned from the war. Ben promptly disappeared on his return only to show up running what could barely be called a motel, stuck off the road somewhere near Carolina Beach.

It was a cool, early morning in October when Ben, unshaven, and balancing a mug of coffee and an already stale donut from the lobby, heard the buzzer announcing someone at the front desk. Odd. Who would call this early? Outside of four business types from New Jersey who had come down the day before to fish, the Sea Oats Motel was empty.

Ben shuffled through the door from his quarters to the front desk to see a small girl with coffee-and-cream-colored skin standing before the counter looking up at him. Behind her stood a tall black woman with the frigid look of detachment in her eyes.

"I thought it about time she met her father," she explained.

Olive Mills cocked her head as if she were just another person anticipating an answer. The features of ancient Africa were on her face. Her stiff, braided hair had been stretched and tied behind her neck with a red ribbon giving her eyes a look of the orient. Her loose fitting dress of rough woven, green wool was gathered at the waist by a hemp rope and she wore the native-woven open sandals. A multi-colored gem necklace hung around her neck. For all of it, nothing could hide the figure behind the dress. She moved forward so her body pressed against the girl.

"This is Rachel," she said.

Ben looked at Olive and then at the child. God, it had been so long. His mind had refused to acknowledge the passing of time. Standing before him was a scene he might see in a movie. Then the reality set in. He was speechless.

"Welcome to my world," he finally said.

That first day, Olive sat on the rear deck and watched Rachel and Ben together as they walked on the beach and picked up shells. Later, she asked each of them if they had fun and wanted to see

41

each other again. Rachel and Ben looked at each other and smiled, and the agreement between Olive and Ben was sealed. Every time Rachel came, Olive would sit on the deck and watch. After several months of watching, one Saturday she left Rachel alone with Ben for several hours while she ran errands. By the time summer came the next year, Rachel was allowed to stay overnight if she wanted; and it was better that way because Ben and Olive didn't have to face each other and try to make conversation.

Ben hired a local high school student to watch the front desk when he knew Rachel was coming. He started to take her along with him in his beat up Ford pickup truck when he ran to the library or shopped at the nearest grocery. At first, Ben didn't know how to act. Being with a mixed race child in public during the late 1940s put not only himself and Rachel, but those around him in an awkward position. But he discovered that he actually enjoyed being a parent, and after a while it became much easier to ignore the stares; and, eventually, the reaction he and Rachel got while out in public didn't bother him anymore.

Ben loved to look at Rachel. Her light cocoa skin and short, curly black hair that sat like a cap on her head were truly striking. Ben's eyes were constantly drawn to the harmonious image she projected: animated hazel eyes set off by brilliant white teeth in a generous mouth, all displayed on a palette of soft brown and supported by a lithe figure and long legs that moved with a grace that matched his own.

Her curiosity about the world around her amazed him. She always had a catalogue of observations and questions, which she constantly threw at him. He did his best to respond to them all, but finally gave up and bought her a used set of encyclopedias.

Rachel's continuing fascination was with the sea and all the living things that made it their home.

"Daddy, what's that thing crawling there that looks like a big flea," she asked on one visit to the beach. "Look, it's burrowing down under the water into the sand."

"Well, it's a crustacean with a fancy name, but that's exactly what they call it, a 'Sand Flea.' We use them as bait for fishing. The fish love them."

Rachel loved to fish. She took to it with an enthusiasm that almost matched his own, wading in the surf and whipping the rod over her right shoulder so that the tackle flew over the waves into the slew beyond. She knew that's where the big fish lay, waiting for their smaller prey to be flushed by the tide into the deeper water. Ben taught her how to filet the fish they kept, and she dressed them out on the water-packed beach sand and threw the remains to the gulls. In the evenings, they fried the fish in hot oil, or broiled them coated with ingredients Ben called his 'secret recipe' and ate together, enjoying each other's company.

The evening of the storm, Sarah had hugged Rachel and kissed Ben, and hurried on her way out into the windy and dark evening. The storm looked like it was picking up speed, and the outer bands were already bringing a spattering of rain. The smell of rain on the ocean and beach was in the air. Ben made a final tour of the motel grounds, tying down garbage cans and stowing loose objects, and returned to watch Rachel throw together a salad and warm up what remained of the stew they had the night before. They ate facing the large, thick, plate glass window that looked out on the angry sea. Ben could handle the small, passing storms that were prevalent this time of year. They had a dark, brooding presence he could identify with; and as quickly as they came they were gone; and there was a new freshness and vibrancy in the air that seemed to impact his life and brighten his mood. This storm was different. Packing a ruthless potential that was palpable to his senses, the feeling was like the violence he knew was coming when he was in the war. Something was going to happen. He could tell.

THE PLOT

Luther sat on the bunk in the dank prison cell, the cheap, thin mattress buckling under his weight. Sagging springs protested loudly at each shift of his body. Normally, his face would be drawn into a tragic mask, the years of confinement, the bleak surroundings, the repetitive work, all weighing heavily on him. But this evening was different. A rare smile, almost a smirk, slowly formed at the corners of his mouth. If things went as planned—and boy, had he worked on this one—Pender, his cellmate, would soon be on his way out of prison, his nude and greased dwarf's body slithering like a snake along a narrow drainage pipe passing under the prison wall. Not hard to accomplish if you were hidden in the prison's newly renovated laundry room where the final construction had just been completed a few hours ago…watching a new drainage system being installed; looking in total disbelief at it being unguarded with only the newly poured concrete to protect it. Of course, no one would ever believe humans could squeeze into a pipe that size, much less knead and bend their body to conform to its twists and turns as they made their way toward a holding pond outside the prison gates. But then no one had ever seen the likes of Pender before.

A Time Before the End

Escape! He'd been thinking about it since the first day they slammed the cell door on him. So had the other cons. Everyone had their own idea about how to break out. Once outside the prison wall, it was how they were going to elude the dogs and cops. Somewhere in the mix was their final destination. For some, it was south of the border, the further south the better. For others, it was to find their way to some far corner of the world and become a soldier of fortune. And then, there were those places that tore men's souls, the places they had lived and left behind—Africa—the Serengeti, sunrise and the essence of life never experienced before; the evenings, after the hunt and the rain, in the tents with their gin and tonic or whatever the hell else they were into. And the women. Oh God, the women. The prison had all kinds of men, and most were doomed to remain there forever. Luther was determined not to be one of them.

Escape! The planning itself always left Luther in a good mood, a state of euphoria even. But when his plans failed to develop Luther hit rock bottom, his depression and unpredictable behavior permeating the cellblock. The experience that changed Luther most came when he escaped from a road gang near a National Forest. The Bloodhounds found him first, and he fought them off with his fists; then the German Shepherds got hold of him, and finally the guards took their Billy Clubs to him. He was a miserable sight being brought through the gates in chains, bloody, soaking wet, helpless, led by several guards he had tried to kill in the melee. Luther was kept in solitary confinement for three months. He had not spoken to a single soul, nor had the guards talked to him except to curse him. Not that any of that meant much to Luther. He hadn't been in solitary confinement before. For the first time, he was absolutely alone in silence with the voices in his head.

He was certain they had always been there, except that sometimes the voices were so disguised he barely recognized them. Were they hidden in the wind as it howled along the ancient pier or whistled through the cracks of the old house or were they the whisper of little mice feet on the linoleum floor in the kitchen? Sometimes the voices seemed to come from the void of the cellblock when

46

darkness finally set in. But then, then, they would come upon him in the night like a stampede, noises in the background at first, and then the increasing pounding sounds of hooves. Voices—raucous, strident, demanding—surrounding him, pounding on him, until they passed and he was left exhausted with nothing remaining except their message.

The voices came to Luther again the night Pender appeared in the prison yard. For the first time since he had heard them they had form, like the shimmer of spider webs with the morning dew on them, or mist rising from the swamp. Except now they were real, whispering in his ear, tempting him, urging him. The time had come to make a final escape attempt; to do it right this time; to do it *their* way.

Escape! Luther sat quietly with his imagination growing and growing until it fulfilled all possibilities—Pender shinnying around the twists and turns of the pipe naked as a jaybird until he came to the holding pond. And then the little devil would . . . would . . . God, to be free at last! Free! How long had it been? Fifteen, sixteen years? And how long since he had seen his Momma? As Luther thought about it, tears streamed from his eyes. He vividly remembered the last time.

In the beginning, when he had first gone away, his Momma, Lenore, visited him every week, making the round trip from Hanover to Raleigh, the pain of the tragic events still on her face. Over time, he could see the changes taking place within her. Sometimes her mind would wander. There would be a blank stare on her face. She couldn't remember. He couldn't stand seeing her like that—the beautiful Lenore with the pale, bloodless face and the sad down-turned green clown eyes and the flowing auburn hair—the one who truly loved him without any reservations. The only time he had cried after child-hood was when his favorite hunting dog died. That was, until that day when his Momma sat across from him, her hair in strings, fumbling with the buttons on her blouse, trying to remember his name. After he returned to his cell, ugly, retching sounds could be heard coming from his bunk.

Suddenly, Lenore stopped coming. Every week he sat hoping a guard would come to escort him to the visitation area where cubicles stood empty and telephones hung silent. A month passed before the guard came to get him.

"They say a pretty woman's waiting out there to see you, Luther," the guard said.

Luther could hardly believe it! Something had happened to make his Momma well. He didn't even complain as the restraints went on around his waist and hands.

When he eased himself onto the cubicle seat, someone other than his Momma sat in front of him. She was indeed a pretty woman, with strawberry blond hair and large indigo blue eyes that nature had mysteriously hidden behind high cheekbones and prominent brows. The years had treated her well, softening her face to highlight its structure and the startling features. Luther's aunt, Becky Porter, studied him from across the cubicle, a look of deep sadness carved on her face.

"What is it, Aunt Becky? What's wrong?" Luther asked. She raised her eyes to his and he captured the lost hope in them.

"Luther, Lenore is in the hospital," Becky said. "She's had what they call a complete mental breakdown. We've had a hard time with her recently. She's been talking to herself and seeing things that aren't there. They're giving her electric shock treatments and drugs, which help, but the symptoms keep coming back. I'm afraid she won't be coming to see you anytime soon. I'm sorry, Luther, I know how much you love her."

No! No one knew how much he loved his Momma, no one except Luther. He couldn't put it into words, but the emotions that raged within and tore at his insides left him helpless, trembling. And, no one understood how much she loved him unless they knew the entire story, and no one did—except Luther.

He knew there was something wrong with him by the time he was old enough to understand what he saw in the mirror. He thought that maybe when he was all dressed up to go out, his looks wouldn't be so scary. Maybe they wouldn't cause people to stare. But he could see the look on their faces and the uncomprehending freak-show shock and fascination of it all. He saw them hug their own children, thankful for their normality, and then their hurrying on as if they could forget it all. If any of it bothered Lenore, she didn't show it. When they heard the whispering, he could feel Lenore draw him close and talk to distract him. When they returned home, she would play the piano and sing to him. Her voice was weak and without resonance, but he listened with rapt attention. To think someone cared enough to sing just for him! Luther had the one thing he knew he could hold on to. He knew his Momma loved him unconditionally. *That would be all he ever needed.*

Escape! Few had made it over the walls to safety, but Luther was different from the rest. He had the, purest, most powerful motivation a man could ever have—to be with the only person on Earth he loved. Until he heard the voices again and regained faith in their reality, he had almost lost hope. But now things were different.

Escape. God, to be free at last. That's where Pender came in. If things went as planned, his greased, naked, scrawny, dwarf's body would be even now emerging from the drainage pipe leading outside the prison wall. When Pender came out the other side, his instructions were simple. With his silent ape skills and particularly his ability to climb and leap, he was to find a way to distract the guard. Luther and the other road gang inmates would do the rest. Then Luther would take his revenge on the people who had kept him from his Momma all these years.

TWO NIGHTMARES

L ike an avalanche roaring down the mountain, the full force of the storm bore down on the small isolated motel. It tore at the siding and storm shutters. It whistled and groaned as it sought entry into any small opening in the structure. It lifted monstrous waves and drove them up the beach into the motel's parking lot. The rain obliterated everything outside, spinning a cocoon of darkness around the motel. Ben's face took on an ashen hue. His hands began to tremble. He abruptly rose from the table.

"Rachel honey," he said in a shaky voice. "I'm going to lie down until this thing blows over. Listen out for the phone. I'm worried about Sarah."

Rachel's smooth brow wrinkled into a frown. She had seen him act like this before, but whatever was causing it had passed, and he had emerged from whatever state he was in with a crooked smile like his old self. But today was different.

Ben went to his bed and pulled back the cover. He lay down and closed his eyes, and listened to the cacophony outside his window.

A Time Before the End

He remembered it as as if it occurred yesterday. It was October 14, 1943 and they had taken off from a remote airstrip near the Parish of Covington in England. The B-17 Flying Fortress, nicknamed "Sadie's Parlor," was one of 291 in formation on their way to bomb the Nazi's ball bearing factories in Schweinfurt, Germany. In the pilot's seat was Captain Edward "Champ" Finley from Nashville, Tennessee. Ben, a lieutenant and Champ's co-pilot, sat to the right of his captain.

Fifty miles out from the target the Messerschmitt and Focke-Wulf fighters broke through the cloud cover and fell on them, their engines screaming as they were revved and approached at full power. Ben heard the nose gunner say "We've got bandits at 12 o'clock," and looked out to see the figure of the German pilot in the fighter as he veered at the last moment. The turret gunners were all yelling, and he could hear the chatter of the .50-caliber machine guns to the rear of him.

When they passed into the target zone, the German fighters retreated, and the cloud-like bursts from the anti-aircraft guns began to fill the sky like puffs from the stems of dandelions. The bombardier was over the Norden bombsight in a compartment forward of the pilot. He said "I've got it Champ," and Champ continued to chew on the dead cigar and Ben sat in the co-pilot's seat helping Champ with the course corrections, and the Flying Fortress shook from the shell bursts.

A red light went on in the instrument panel and the plane shimmied and rose free of its six thousand pounds of bombs, and the bombardier called "bombs away." When they passed over the target zone all noise stopped except for the sound of the four Wright turbocharged engines. Again the German fighters came after them, and Ben could see the wreckage in the sky. Bombers were on fire, aircraft parts were falling around them like boulders being dropped by some crazed giant, and now, parachutes were floating down. With a shudder, "Sadie's Parlor" was hit. Smoke began to pour from the inboard starboard engine and Ben shut it down. "We've got a bandit closing in at 6 o'clock high," the tail gunner said, and then he said "Oh" and was silent.

The outboard starboard engine was on fire now and belching smoke. Ben shut it down but the fire burned on. The plane began to lose altitude, and Champ said over the intercom, "We're not going to make it. You guys get ready to jump."

Ben pushed himself erect and looked at Champ. "I think they got Phil. I'm going back to check." Ben lost his balance and crawled monkey style to the rear. Phil Hester lay extended behind his machine gun, his bloodied head to one side, his only visible eye staring at nothing. Ben broke the chain holding Phil's dog tags and stuck them in his pocket. When he turned to go back he could see the crew one by one pushing themselves through the open hatch. The B-17 was banking to one side in the beginning throes of a death spiral when Ben got back and found Champ's hand waiting for him, pulling him forward.

Ben glanced out the hatch and saw the Messerschmitt fighters circling in the distance.

"Go ahead, Champ," Ben said. "I got to get this chute strap fixed. I'm right behind you."

Was something wrong with Ben's chute strap? The crew had checked each other's packs before takeoff. Champ gave Ben a funny look and pushed himself out. Ben continued to hold onto the hatch watching Champ fall. He knelt hunched at the opening. He couldn't move. He was frozen in place, trembling, terrified. Suddenly the plane began to roll and Ben found himself falling forward. His body cleared the plane's tail section and he found the parachute ripcord and pulled it.

The noise from the storm pounded the house. Ben lay in the bed and began to sweat. Even in the act of remembrance his fear of falling turned his body as rigid as if it had been in the final stages of rigor mortis.

Ben was drifting in the cloudless, noonday sky and could see the crew with their arms above their heads gripping their parachute harnesses and floating downwind. In the sky below to his right was Champ, and beyond him, five specks closing fast. The Messerschmitt 109s banked and circled the airmen. Then, with a tip of their wings they attacked. Ben heard the planes firing and watched his buddies' arms drop and bodies twitch and fall limp at their sides. A single Messerschmitt turned towards Ben and Champ. Ben pulled frantically on the parachute lines to slip the 'chute to the right and then rock it back to the left, trying to escape the fury coming at him. A short burst from the guns tore into the chute like the sound of a boxer hitting a punching bag. The chute swirled and Ben dropped his arms and head as if he were hit. Then he heard the plane fire again, and when he looked down Champ's body was like the others, and the German pilot was banking the Messerschmitt and headed toward other specks in the endless sky beyond. Ben was left alone looking at his buddies in their chutes, their heads and arms flopping like marionettes with broken strings. They were all dead. Only Ben was left.

Rachel had moved from the table to the couch when she heard the screams.

Ben had remembered the electrodes attached between his thighs. "Nooo...God...please, nooo! Oh, please don't do that to me."

She had heard sounds coming from his room before, but nothing this intense and terror filled. The noise rose to a crescendo and then fell like the resonance from a cannon roar until only the sucking intake of air could be heard.

Rachel ran to Ben's room. He lay there, his body still rigid, trembling, gasping, a rattling sound coming from deep inside. She threw herself on top of him.

"Daddy!" she screamed. "What's wrong, Daddy! Please don't die, please!"

She laid there, her hands grasping his head, trying to stop the spasms. Her tears fell on his face and into his open mouth.

"Please, daddy! Please!"

Responding to her cries, his body slowly loss its rigor mortis-like stiffness. His eyes began to blink. He looked up into her terrified face.

"Water. I need some water," he said.

When she returned with the glass, he was sitting on the side of the bed. The sheet was saturated with sweat everywhere she saw the imprint of his body and the pungent odor of urine perfumed the air.

Ben stood in the middle of the kitchen, his hands trembling, trying to control a cup of coffee. Rachel stood near the sink, a wash towel twisted in her hands, her face red and contorted from what she had seen.

"I love you Daddy," she said. She didn't know what else to say.

The storm's front had passed, leaving only the remnants of its force—a groaning sound and the dying wind and rain.

Ben continued to stand, breathing heavily, waiting for the trauma to dissipate. Suddenly, he heard a noise coming from outside. There was a force pushing at the door. Was it someone caught by the storm that couldn't reach the lobby, or maybe his only guests, the fishermen, who had been unable to reach him? Or was it's the storms last desperate stab at trying to search for and destroy him?

While his tortured mind was trying to react, a man and a woman burst through the door. Despite protection by their windbreakers, they were thoroughly soaked, their hair dripping and plastered to their heads. Their eyes had the look of fugitives being pursued.

Sarah ran straight to Ben, wrapping her arms around him.

"We couldn't reach you," she cried. "We were afraid . . . " Her voice trailed off.

Ben looked at the man standing before him. He was the largest, most muscular, meanest looking black man he had ever seen—his skin almost purple in the dim light of the room, the stark whiteness of his eyes marked by tiny red capillaries that stood out like stripes from a switch, his face scarred and pitted from fights and smallpox.

"Mr. Ben, Miss Sarah and me, we worried sick about you," he said in a strained but gentle voice.

Ben had known him since childhood. "Black James" was the only name he was known by then, and he liked it that way. Liquor, women, and a sharp knife, had gotten James in more trouble than you could shake a stick at, as folks were wont to say. His body was as hard as a rock from slinging a sledgehammer. When he didn't show up at your door asking for something to eat, you knew he was on a chain gang somewhere.

Miss Carly Delome, the local mystic and "Voodoo Healer," as she called herself, knew he was a gentle giant when he wasn't drinking, and one day decided it was time for James to straighten up. She pulled him into the room with the African masks and the dolls. When he came out his giant body was shaking; there was a look akin to terror in his eyes. From that day on he was a changed man. He became known as "Miss Carly's man, 'Black James.'" Nobody messed with Miss Carly!

With the storm receding, Sarah clinging to him and Black James towering over him, Ben tried to pull himself together.

"James, something's wrong. Tell me, please," he said in an uneven voice.

James moved even closer. He looked down into Ben's ravaged face. He laid his hand gently on his shoulder.

"Mr. Ben, Miss Carly call me at Pauline's. She be real upset. I tell Miss Sarah, but your phone be out. That why we here. Miss Carly say you got to bring Miss Rachel to her place now. Miss Olive be there. Sheriff Tindal coming."

"For God's sake James. Why? What's wrong!" Ben cried.

"Mr. Luther, he break out of jail. They say he headed this way. Say he coming to see his Momma and kill you and Miss Olive.

56

Miss Rachel in danger too. That what they say." James' deep and resonant voice echoed in the still, silent room.

In shock, Ben stepped away from Sarah and James. Luther loose! Coming this way! Dread took over Ben's emotions—terror-laden thoughts going round and round in his mind like rats on a treadmill. He was suddenly as frightened as he had ever been in the war; afraid not for himself alone, but for Olive and their child Rachel and for Sarah. With Luther locked away, he thought the madness of the past and what had happened so long ago in Dry Pond was behind him. He wanted to believe that after the war and the hospitals and the doctors, he was on the road to getting his life back together; that he might finally be healed in mind, body and spirit. Now, with Luther free and bent on killing all of them, he didn't see how he could take any more storms in his life, at least not without breaking.

THE ROOM

The storm was blowing itself out up the coast over Topsail Beach when Ben Porter turned his Ford pickup off the black top onto a hard packed dirt road. Where the road was worn, it had a washboard effect on the old truck's suspension system, but with all the vibration Ben's hands still remained steady on the wheel. His intense emotions had calmed significantly from the ones experienced back at the motel, and he had now fallen into an alert silence. Rachel sat with a solemn expression, her arms wrapped around her body. Two hundred yards of bouncing brought Ben to a graveled entrance covering a drainage ditch. He wheeled to a stop in front of a small yellow house with a tin roof. A covered porch ran the length of the front. A two-person swing hung at one end. He knew the house intimately, having been in and out of it in his youth more times than he could count. The house had been enlarged to add another room and bath, but he knew he could walk through it blindfolded and place every item close to its original location . . . especially in *The Room*.

Sarah and Black James had already arrived. They stood on the porch waiting. So did Olive Mills. She stood straight with her hands clasped in front. Despite the chill of an evening whose sky still reflected the last rays of the dying sun, she wore a thin, variegated cotton print dress that the remaining wind imprinted on her body. Rachel jumped down and ran to Olive. There were no words. In the midst of danger, holding each other was enough.

Ben stood beside the front fender of the old Ford trying to bring everything that had happened into perspective. Imprinted in his memory was the story of *The Room* he was about to enter.

If you had been standing in the crowd that chilly November evening more than twenty years ago, you could easily have overlooked her. She was as nondescript in her domestic maid's clothing as any of the other black housemaids, her head covered by a colorful scarf, carrying a bag of cleaning items—just a tired domestic worker on her way home followed by two young people pushing each other as they moved along. But there was something about the woman's carriage, the way she carried herself that distinguished her from the other maids.

"You two stop messing with each other and come along," Carly Delome said.

"You stop pushing now, white boy," Olive said.

"Now you know his name is Ben," the woman young Ben Porter called Miss Carly pointedly said.

Olive grinned mischievously. "I know, but I still wants to call him white boy."

Ben smiled. It was Olive's way of saying she liked him. They had been thrown together ever since that fateful day at the lake when his mother Becky had offered Miss Carly a room in the house until she could get settled, and Carly had insisted on keeping house and doing chores to pay for her and Olive's keep. Ben had grown to like the way Olive talked up to him and teased him with a knowing smile. A bond had grown between the thin, blond white boy and the long legged chocolate-colored girl.

Carly led Ben and Olive to a wooded rise looking down on a

plateau where people were gathering in preparation for what looked like a celebration. Folks with ornately decorated masks were already getting in line and performers from a circus group were arriving.

The event was an annual fall celebration in a part of town largely inhabited by poor blacks and whites caught up together in the poverty of the Depression. Usually it was an unplanned, almost spontaneous event, the date passed on by word of mouth to the residents who lived at the base of the huge depression in the floor of the earth called Dry Pond. This year, things would be different. Miss Carly had volunteered to plan and manage the event, and everyone knew what that meant. With Miss Carly running things, it was certain to be a grand occasion. Recalling the lore of her African ancestors, she drew on an ancient ceremony dating back over a thousand years known as the *Fetes des Masques* or Festival of Masks. Originally, new masks were created each year and worn in contests to determine the best dancers. Tribes would compete and festivals would last for a week or more. On the last day one of the masks would be chosen as a winner and buried as a tribute to the spirits who were always thought to be present.

Suddenly the action started. Round and round the dancers whirled as they circled the tall totem-like pole, weaving in and out like a snake in motion to the intoxicating rhythm of the bongo drums. Their singing and dancing filled the chilly, dry night as if the evening itself were alive. Some of the dancers wore masks; others shook them in their hands like tambourines. On and on the dancers whirled, their arms batting the air as if they were warding off a horde of insects. When some dropped out of line from fatigue others took their places—a racial mixture of women with their men and children, all celebrating in the ritual. An albino man joined the line, his skin like a smattering of white paint against the dark background. To Benjamin Porter who had recently celebrated his thirteenth birthday, it was a sight to behold.

Slowly, the opening ceremony ran down, and the tired but happy dancers departed or sat down on the bed of recently spread pine straw to rest. The circus performers looked with expressions that clearly said, "We can outdo that."

Another kind of ceremony would come later that evening with similar yet frightening overtones. It was called Voodoo.

"Come along now," Miss Carly ordered pulling them away from the opening toward a disordered collection of shanties lying like tossed pebbles along the dirt road leading out of the valley towards town. "I got to get dressed and come back to take care of some matters. Tomorrow's going to be a busy day for all of us because the circus is going to perform and ya'll got to be ready early."

When they got to the small yellow house, more like a shack than anything else, Miss Carly carefully unlocked the door and ushered Ben and Olive into a small room.

Ben had never been inside the room. He had heard rumors, but he was unprepared for what he saw. When he stepped over the doorsill, his mouth fell open, his startled eyes fixed as if he had seen an apparition. He had never seen a room decorated like this before.

The top of the walls were strung with rows of beads separated by tiny, multicolored lights whose radiance was caught by the beads and exploded into a galaxy of Roman candle colors. The rear wall was split by a doorway, hung with a colorful curtain of tinkling glass ornaments, which served as a pass-through to the rest of the house.

On the left side of the rear wall hung an elegant but sinister looking large necklace made of animal bones filed to shape and interspersed with a flawless array of gleaming wolf fangs. On the right an assortment of African tribal masks were affixed to the wall in an oblique pattern from top to bottom. A large knife in its sheaf whose handle looked as if it might be gold was attached in a horizontal position. Waiting to be lighted, votive candles rested in small alcoves along the sidewalls of the room. On two shelves, one on the right and one on the left, sat an assortment of hand made dolls, each face delicately painted to show the emotions of that particular face. In the middle of the room stood a plain pine table empty except for an uncut deck of Tarot cards in the middle. To one side stood a cabinet filled with bottles of powders and portions of various hues.

Ben broke out of his reverie to look up on the porch at Olive.

"Hi, white boy," she said, and Ben knew they were still friends despite what had happened to their relationship.

Ben walked up the steps and kissed Rachel, Olive, and Sarah on the cheek.

Inside the Room, Ben stopped, his feet frozen in place as if he had heard a command. It was as he thought. The interior had changed very little over the years.

There were a row of folding chairs set up facing the door, and everyone sat, including Becky Porter and Sheriff Buck Tindal. Miss Carly sat with her back to the door facing the group.

"Sheriff, you want to go first," she said.

Buck Tindal rose quickly, and moved to the table facing the group. He walked on the balls of his feet, toes forward, a cross in stance between an Indian tracking a wounded animal and a wrestler advancing toward his opponent. He had been a high school wrestling champ before he was a soldier and then a sheriff, and had tracked many a bootlegger to a still site without cracking a twig. He was slightly under six feet, but the years had drawn him down a bit, and the biceps and thighs that once had flexed through his clothing like an Iguana's swollen throat had now begun to lose some of their texture. Still, they had the quality of intimidating anyone he was about to arrest, and if that didn't impress them, the black patch he wore over his left eye would.

"OK, everyone. If you can, rest at ease. We need clear heads. By now, you all know that Luther has escaped and killed a guard doing it. All the signs indicate he's headed this way. They think he's with an ex-sideshow performer, a short, ape-like looking guy named Pender Hicks. Told everybody he's going to kill us all or all he can get to. State Police are all over it. They've got roadblocks blocking every highway between Raleigh and here, and Brunswick County and us got our own people out guarding the rural and city highways. And, we've got police guarding each of your homes; and Ben, your motel. Not much else we can do. Everybody needs to be on the alert, and if you've got a gun, so much the better. I'll take questions later, but Miss Carly's got something to say to you all."

Like an eagle rising to leave her nest, Carly slowly pushed her aging body from the chair. Despite the extra pounds the years had added and health problems, she moved in the rhythmic gait of a jungle animal, her primal energy radiating in waves with each step. The beauty she once possessed was now chiseled beneath the flesh of her aging face like the form of a mask to which a makeup artist had plied his trade. She stood beside Sheriff Tindal and the table with the tarot cards. She waited a moment until all eyes including the Sheriff's were fixed on hers.

"I have had restless nights and bad dreams," she said bluntly. The Petro, the evil spirits of Voodoo, who disappeared for so long have returned. I have known them in my dreams, heard their voices. Again they are legion and I am unable to cast them out. The sweet Rada, the good spirits, do not have the power to oppose them. The evil spirits travel with Luther. He must be slain to destroy the curse. You remember: *"There will be madness, murder, and mayhem."* Our only hope is what the good spirits, the Rada, added: *"finally, a savior will appear, at a time before the end."*

"We do not know who that person will be and when that time will come, so we must all be vigilant. I have dealt the tarot cards you see here, and there is a disturbing trend."

Carly shuffled the tarot deck once more and gave one left to right face down to each person present.

"Now, turn them over. Who has card thirteen?" she asked.

The first person she had delivered a card to was Ben. He raised his hand.

"What do you see?" Carly asked.

Ben looked at the card, then answered.

"It shows a picture of death as a skeleton dressed in black armor riding a white steed. He is carrying some kind of pennant. At his feet is a child begging for mercy and another looking away in despair. A king or a pontiff of some sort is standing in front of the skeleton and appears to be begging the Death figure to spare his people. Under the horse's feet is a body face down."

Carly took the card from Ben and passed it in turn to each person in the room.

"This is what we are all facing," she said.

PART TWO

CARLY'S STORY

HAITI 1895

"*Carly, leve, leve vit!*" Binta Dohou said in Creole as she shook the child.

Startled, the child sat upright and rubbed her eyes. Her caramel coloring was in sharp contrast to the woman looking down at her. She looked into her mother's black face and saw fear in the white of her stark round, eyes, fear like that of a gazelle facing an approaching lion on the African plains.

"Momma, Momma, sak gen-yen?"

"*Carly, nou gen pwoblem. Fok nou pati.* We must leave. There is news of a revolt against the government in Port-au-Prince. Charles fears for himself and the children. They are leaving tonight. We must go alone."

"*Men Momma*, why can't we go with them?"

Binta puts her finger to Carly's lips. She would have to learn the truth later. There was no time to waste.

"Because it's not possible. Now, let's get your things together. We must go before it's too late."

The reality that the child and she would have to stay behind in the path of the rampaging rebels was the most horrifying moment in Binta's life. The echoes of Charles words were still in her head.

Charles Delome was standing, facing the large sitting room, his attention seemingly on a mural depicting a rural scene: a French nobleman in royal blue riding attire astride a large white horse with a standard black poodle standing at its front feet. It was a picture of him, Charles, a young aristocrat, taken outside Paris in his early twenties.

He was turning to face Binta as he spoke, his eyes now fixed on the wall behind her, his chin lifted so that it pulled his skin tight in a pose he often showed in his negotiations with the government officials in Port-au-Prince.

"Binta, the children and I are returning to France. You know how it is here now with the Rebels. Nothing has been stable since the revolt." His cultured French was like a song in the stillness of the room.

"I regret that I cannot take you and Carly with me. We've talked about it before. Port-au-Prince is one thing. Paris is another. As my consort, you are in grave danger here. You and Carly must leave immediately."

Binta's face took on the startled look of one being suddenly slapped. For a moment that seemed endless, she was speechless.

The protective presence of the plantation was all Binta had known, rarely leaving for an occasional trip to Port-au-Prince with Charles to be displayed as a test of his sensitivity to ethnic influences within the government. Binta's mother, Zinsa, had been captured from her home in Dahomey, West Africa, and brought by slave traders to Haiti. Sold to a wealthy French plantation owner, she worked in the sugarcane fields until her death under the sweltering heat that always rested like a blanket on the plantation during the summer. Binta was saved from the same fate only by her great beauty and the seductive aura she carried as if it were a parasol. When the new plantation owner, a widower named Charles Delome came down with a fever that was ravaging the country, he called for Binta as his nurse. Soon after his recovery, he took her to his bed. When Carly was born, Binta was allowed to bring her into the mansion where, with Charles own children, she was schooled by a French tutor; and where Binta learned enough French to preside over the household servant-slaves and serve as an occasional escort for Charles. Now, in the blink of an eye, all that was changed. When she finally spoke, Binta's pained voice was like the whimper of a frightened child.

"Charles, where will we go? We have always lived here."

With a turn of his hand, Charles dismissed her concerns.

"Jean-Paul will take you with him. I have paid him well."

Jean-Paul was a native who had ears in the inter-sanctum of the President's council. Charles had advanced him a handsome retainer for his services that had paid off richly until the rebels had overrun the city's defenses and the government itself was under siege. Charles' political dealings with regime changes in Haiti were well known and understood; but Jean-Paul's drunken, boastful babbling to a paid rebel prostitute that Charles was financially contributing to the government's efforts to squash the uprising was a fatal blow to his chances of staying above the conflict. The Catholic Clergy, ministering to the French, had been warned and many had fled the island. Plantation owners were scrambling to appease the Rebels if they could, or running if they couldn't. But Charles Delome didn't have a choice. The Rebels had sworn bloody revenge on him and his family and that included Binta and Carly.

Jean-Paul, who had been standing just outside the door listening, entered the room with a flourish and a look of embarrassment on his face. He spoke in a purring obsequious voice.

"Monsieur, my apologies for being late," he said as he turned to face Binta.

"Binta, it will be difficult to take you entirely beyond the reach of the Rebels," he said. We cannot travel fast enough together because, you know, the child. They will rape you and Carly and make me watch and then kill us all. They are animals. I have a cousin, Saintael, who lives in the village of Sucre, near the city of Gonavies. He is a *Houngan*; you know, a Voodoo priest, and his wife Patrice a *Mambo*, a priestess. They will hide you and Carly. The rebels are superstitious swine. They will not invade the sacred ceremonial grounds."

71

Binta and Carly arrived in Sucre under cover of night. To throw the Rebels off track, they were quickly separated and given new identities. Carly remained with Saintael and Patrice, posing as their only child. Binta became one of the soiled field workers living in a hut near the village. Jean-Paul was right; the Rebels bypassed Sucre, carrying their thirst for blood to more important sites.

During the long hot days of Summer, Carly would often sit with Patrice under the shade of the great Lemba tree whose giant roots provided seating in the middle of the Sucre temple yard where the Voodoo ceremonies were held. From Patrice, Carly learned about the history of the Voodoo religion. How it had its roots in Africa as spirit worship, but came into its own in Haiti when slaves were not allowed by the Church and their masters to practice it. But the slaves were not easily deterred. They created a cover to fool the Catholic Church, an amalgamation of African spirit worship and Catholic ritual. Virtually all African spirits, called Loa, were associated with Catholic Saints, so slaves could celebrate and commune with their Loa under the cover of the Catholic ceremony. When the slaves were finally able to bring the practice of their faith outside the Church, it evolved into a new religion with its own ceremonial rites named Voodoo.

Binta and Carly lived near the small village of Sucre for twelve years. They worked as laborers during the season harvesting sugarcane, cacao beans, sisal, and preparing the skins of vetiver, limes, amyris, and bitter orange to be made into perfumes, soaps, and ointments. Year by year, layer by layer, the veneer of privileged living inside the Plantation mansion was stripped off until only their sweat-covered bodies and boundless, unfettered, native spirit remained. Each year during the fifteen-day Voodoo ceremonial holiday at Sucre, Binta and Carly danced to the intoxicating rhythms of the Bongo drums and thanked the sweet Loa for their deliverance.

Carly was eighteen and working in the fields when Binta approached her. Binta had only grown more beautiful with time.

Her noble African face had softened somewhat, but the high cheek-bones under dark, sultry eyes and sculptured, pouting lips remained. She was sought by many men, and judged each according to the standards of "goodness" she had set.

Binta laid her hands on Carly's shoulders and drew her into an embrace. When she released her, she fixed her eyes on Carly's face

"Carly, after much thought I have decided to marry Phillipe. Perhaps he is not who I would have chosen when I was so young and passionate, but he has been good to both of us and he wants me, you know. Phillipe says we will always be poor if we continue to live here. He wants us to move to the city of Miami in Florida. He has an uncle there. We have a letter from him."

Binta held up a soiled piece of paper filled with a hopeful description of what awaited them when they moved to Miami. There was a small Haitian community that was growing larger with each new uprising on the island. Phillipe had worked as a chef in a private club in Port-au-Prince before the latest uprising and slaughter and had barely escaped with the clothing on his back. Surely he could find a job at one of the fine restaurants in the city of Miami or the new hotels being built at the beach. In time they might open their own café. Binta held the letter to her breasts as if it were a guarantee of happiness and prosperity.

"Carly, Phillipe has saved enough to buy us all tickets on the boat. We leave next week."

Carly's dress was soaked from the intense heat of mid-day. The cotton work frock clung to her body as if it were a wet piece of thin paper. Her hair fell onto her face in long, damp, black strands. When she turned to face her mother, an expression of apprehension and sadness had colored her face. It was only last night that she had a dream in which she felt the presence of her special spirit, the earth mother, *Erzulie*. There was something *Erzulie* was telling her about Binta, something unsettling, and Carly woke up in a sweat with a deep feeling of foreboding.

Tears flooded Carly's face.

"Momma, I cannot go with you," she said. "For me the signs are not good. You know I have been a *serviteur* in the faith for some time, and now have been invited to participate in the *Kanzo* ceremony and prepare to become a priestess. Voodoo has taken over my life. The other *Houngans* and *Mambos* think I have a special talent. There is so much work to be done here. You see it—the hunger, the disease, the dying babies. The old ones, they sit in the streets alone, begging and crying. And think of the many others who need help and faith. For all of them, I must stay. Perhaps the good Loa spirits will allow me to come later."

Binta's face tightened. The two had drawn as close as sisters by their shared adversity. The thought of leaving Carly behind overwhelmed her. She took Carly into her arms again.

"I love you so much, Carly," she cried.

Binta backed slowly away with her hand to her mouth and her eyes filled with tears. When she could no longer tolerate the sight of Carly looking so forlorn, standing in the field alone, she turned and ran.

During the following weeks, Carly reflected on the meaning of the abrupt and painful separation from her mother. They had the tickets! She could have gone on to a new life and away from the filth, the poverty, the disease. Why didn't she? In a series of haunting dreams, the answer finally arrived: The overwhelming mystery of Voodoo—its powers invested in the living spirits of nature, the Loa, who surrounded and communed with her as she reached out to them with her newly acquired skills; the frightening possibility of closeness to the creator of all things—the remote and inscrutable *Bondye*. Zeal for union with these unknowable forces had eaten her up. She began to fast until her bones were like hard sticks punching at her skin. Villagers came out to look as she walked the streets at night, her hands ever reaching for someone or something never there. Her speech was beyond comprehension, filled with gibberish, guttural and harsh. She became a total stranger to those around her. Alarmed and frightened, her friends— *serviteurs* in the Faith— realized she was truly obsessed and helpless.

"She will never become a Mambo now, but we must still save her," the leader of the group said.

Like vigilantes they came in the night and carried her away.

THE CEREMONY

The insistent beat of the Congo drums penetrated the night with their intoxicating, steady rhythm. A determined group of men and women in colorful, festive dress pulled and dragged the struggling woman towards the large, erect, phallus-looking pole rising through the ground fog. Called the *Poto Mitan* by Voodoo worshippers, it was decorated with ancient African symbols and placed in the middle of a circle that represented the center of the universe. All the dancing would take place around it.

Carly Delome, who had fought the rescuing group of *serviteurs* every step of the way, now hung exhausted in their arms. Her eyes, however, were still wild with the look of one possessed. Taking a hemp rope used to harness oxen, they lashed her to the *Poto Mitan*.

The sound of the drums had carried the night and filtered into the surrounding countryside. The villagers, most all except the old and the very young, roused from their sleep by the rhythmic, sensuous beat, were suddenly aware of what would soon be happening. They hastily donned clothes and headed for the event.

When the crowd had assembled, they stared in amazement at the woman bound to the pole. She was struggling, saliva running from her mouth, the tendons in her throat, arms, and legs taut with the adrenaline rush through her body. One of her arms had worked free and she was gesturing at the crowd.

"Look how she only uses her left hand," said a man with a mask that featured a hawk's beak for a nose. Black magic Voodoo was performed only with the left hand, all good Voodoo used the right.

"She is possessed by *Kalfu*," said a wizened crone of a woman, referring to the Petro spirit of the night, the origin of all darkness in nature and the soul.

Like a mongoose sizing up a viper for the kill, adventurous natives edged ever closer to the frothing woman at the stake. To the delight of the crowd, a small boy raced forward to touch her then ran back displaying his finger as if he had touched a sacred object.

A shout was heard from the rear of the crowd. "Burn her at the *Poto Mitan* before she puts a hex on us all."

"But she has always been with us, working to help," replied one of the *serviteur* Voodoo practitioners.

"We have the *Mambos* and the *Houngans* to help us," the voices shouting louder now. "She is dangerous. Kill her."

A man of medium build, cleanly shaven except for a full moustache, waded through the crowd. His cheeks had the long vertical creases that fasting had etched on them like fissures from an earthquake. His eyes were small horizontal slits in a narrow, horse-shaped face. He was dressed in loose white pants tied with a blood red sash and cinched at the knee with a cord of the same color. In his right hand he carried a long sword sharpened on both sides.

The crowd began to whisper his name until the sound reached a roar.

"Georges! It is Georges!"

Georges was the most renowned of all *Houngans* in Haiti, and presided over the annual festival at Sucre. He was seldom seen except at festivals and was said to live in a hidden cave in the mountainous area. He was always seen attended by a giant zombie-like albino with prominent pink eyes. No one knew his real name but he was called Ougoun. The most fervent practitioners of Voodoo thought Ougoun was a real zombie—an old friend of Georges who had died violently and been brought back to life by Georges' occult powers, except Georges had been unable to restore Ouguon's voice because of the evil powers of the Petro spirits. Others thought Ouguon was a real person who had been afflicted since birth, which was the reason he walked like a stereotype of a zombie with an uneven gate and arms stretched forward at shoulder level as if he were going to attack whoever was in his path. Most likely he had been abandoned as a child and by some miracle had survived. People had seen him wandering the hills, gesticulating like a mad man, his appearance with its wild bushy hair and haunted eyes frightening to all but maybe Georges who had obviously claimed him as his own. The real truth about Ougoun remained unknown since he could not speak and Georges would not tell.

As Georges cleared the crowd, he headed straight to Carly. When he was facing her, he raised the sword with both hands.

"The *Houngan* is going to sacrifice her," said a gnarled old man in the crowd. The crowd cheered because the ceremonial dance could not begin before the sacrifice was made.

As Georges flashed the sword in front of Carly, the crowd roared. Something else was happening.

It was Ouguon! He was there! Ouguon came forth dressed only in a loincloth, leading a goat, a kid. The goat was not pulling, but walking placidly, its eyes straight ahead. Georges stood still, poised, waiting, Carly and the dumb animal now standing before him. The albino stood to the side with his pink eyes fixed on Carly. The crowd fell silent.

A guttural sound came from Ouguon as he dropped the tether holding the goat. Neither a crack of a limb, a muffled cough nor even the call of an animal came from the surrounding area. All was still.

Standing between the goat and Carly and waving the sword over both their heads, Georges paused and turned to the crowd.

"Which one do you want me to sacrifice," he said.

Many shouted loudly. "Kill her." Others who knew of her good works protested. Georges hesitated. The suspense grew. Then, swifter than an arrow flies he drew the sword downward onto the goat's neck. It fell without a sound, its neck severed. The sacrifice was completed. "Bondye Bon," Georges whispered. "God is good." To the followers of Voodoo, the killing of an animal in a ceremony does not signify death but is instead the transfer of the life force of the animal to the Loa, the spirits, who expend so much energy as forces of nature they need many such sacrifices to sustain themselves. At the sight before them, the crowd went into a frenzy, some screaming and tearing at their clothes, others swooning and falling to the ground. The Congo drums exploded into a wild, prolonged beat. The crowd quickly formed a circle and began to dance around the *Poto Mitan.* They sang and chanted to the spellbinding rhythm that seemed to overpower them. They weaved in and out shaking their bodies and waving their arms. Some began to bend over from the waist as if the weight of a rider were on their backs. The sounds of strange tongues tore from their lips.

"The Loa are beginning to ride them," said one of the women in white, the *Hounsi,* who were serving ladies who ministered to the needs of the dancers after they had been stricken. The *Hounsi* and many believed that when Loa mount a person, they take over the person's body and mind. The Loa becomes the person. When they leave, something of the Loa's spirit is left to guide the person. *Mambos* and *Houngans* interpret the event and help the person understand the message.

Georges drew his body close to Carly. "The power of the snake is with me," he said, as if talking to himself. He was referring to *Dumballah,* the good snake, a powerful symbol in Voodoo. "Do exactly as I say and you will be safe," he whispered as he cut the ropes. "The mob has their sacrifice and are already into the dance. You must participate. When they drink the Klerin they will go crazy and harm you if you are not one of them."

The shock of the events had driven the wildness from Carly's eyes although she worried that the strong drink might convince them to kill her. She nodded at Georges. Taking her by the hand, he pulled her into the ring of frenzied dancers. She knew the steps and moves of the ritual from the many times she had participated, and was at once part of the delirium taking place around her. Someone poured Klerin on her head and it ran down her face, seeping into her mouth.

Suddenly, she threw back her head, lifted her arms and began to groan as if she were in intense agony. Immediately she was seized and fell to the ground. When she rose she was bent at the waist as if a heavy weight or rider were on her back. She staggered forward a few feet and fell again. She started to kick and pull at her hair. A third time she tried to rise but could not get to her feet.

"There must be many Loa on her back," said one of the *Hounsi*.

"I have never seen anyone like this," said another. "Something unusual is happening."

Three of the *Hounsi* ran to attend her, but Georges stopped them.

"Let the Loa finish with her," he said.

Carly was writhing where she lay in the dirt and still trying to rise when she was again violently driven to the ground.

When she finally lay prostrate and still, the *Hounsi* went and attended to her, washing her face and combing her hair. After the dancers began to tire and stood catching their breath and the provocative beat of the drums began to fade, Georges came to Carly. He took her by the hand and led her to stand beside the *Poto Mitan*.

"Ougoun!" he shouted.

The crowd began to cry out and hastily pushed each other aside to make a wide pathway. Coming towards them, arms outstretched and walking as if he had just risen from a mummy's crypt, was Ougoun. As he moved directly towards Carly, Georges vanished into the crowd. Carly stood motionless as Ougoun approached. When he stood before her he grasped her head with both hands and began to force his thumbs into her mouth. His mouth was open and his tongue was twisted and thrusting toward her face. Saliva poured from his mouth and he began to make a guttural noise that sounded like a person being choked.

Carly felt intense pressure on her head and his thumbs beginning to tear at her mouth. Strangely, she felt unafraid. Something indefinable, was forcing its way into her mind; a sensation that carried a message even though there were no words. She knew what to do! She placed one hand on top of the other and thrust them over Ougoun's slobbering mouth as if she were trying to hush a child. His pink eyes opened wide and began to protrude. His body began to shake. He fell and lay at Carly's feet.

"*Mambo...Mambo*," he said.

Those were Ougoun's first spoken words.

Carly awoke in her bed with the sun streaming through the window. It must be late in the morning, she thought. She realized she was nude and lying under a sheet. Her clothes were stacked in a neat pile on the floor. The strong smell of *Klerin* was in the room. "Funny, I rarely drink," she said to herself. Then she remembered having the nightmare. A stillness came over her. A membrane between her and the great Bondye had become so thin she could see beyond herself. She was dumbstruck.

Carly bathed and dressed and stepped out into the dirt road that ran by her small house. She walked toward the village and when she got near people were in the street looking at her and staring. Others drew back to make a path. All had a look of astonishment on their faces. An old woman with a goiter on her neck came forward and touched her.

"*Mambo*, heal me," she said.

LEAVING HAITI

When word of the approaching storm came, Carly and a team of volunteers quickly gathered what they could and hiked to the highest ground they could reach and set up a makeshift camp.

When the storm hit the next morning, the water in the Bay of Gonaives curled up its angry tongue and spit its fury at the town. A flood struck the docks and piers and boats and carried the debris on its crest into the town itself. The winds destroyed the flimsy wood and thatch buildings and blew off the roofs and smashed the windows of what was left. The people tried to flee to the higher ground but the mudslides from the deforested hills destroyed the roads and poured into the town. Muck from the water and mud covered everything. There was total devastation. Rescuers could not reach the town until late the next day, and then they seemed to trickle down from the hills like grains of sand from an hourglass.

Carly and the team of volunteers hiked down a remote twisting path through the woods that remained on the hills. They stayed for two weeks burying the dead, tending to the sick and injured, and helping to dig the town out from the mud. When the others were ready to leave, Carly stood before them.

"I have decided Gonaives will be my *hounfo.*" She wanted

81

this parish to be under her influence as a mambo. "I will remain here to help those who need me."

Carly lived in a small hut near the bay, which she turned into an aid station. She slept on a cot behind a curtain so she could always be available to the people. Mambo Carly quickly became renowned as a healer and one whose visions came from somewhere above the terrestrial plain.

One stifling, humid afternoon a knock came on Carly's door.

"Mambo Carly. It is Maya. I have urgent news."

When Carly opened the door, she saw the pain on the face of one of her mother's closest friends.

"I have learned from a messenger that your mother is gravely ill," Maya said. "They did not know how to find you."

Carly's face was covered with sweat from the savage summer heat. Exhaustion showed in her posture and movements. She stood like an ancient gladiator, slumped and completely drained from the fight.

"What is wrong with her, Maya? Tell me." Carly's voice could not contain her fear.

"The doctor's think it is something wrong with her liver. She is wasting away day by day. They do not think she will live long. They want you to come now."

Phillipe met Carly at the dock in Miami. His brown skin had been burned almost black from daily exposure to the sun. His clothes were stained and tattered. His shoulders were bowed.

Phillipe's dream had come to naught. He could not find work as a chef in the fancy restaurants at Miami Beach or in the city. They said his skills were not what they needed. Perhaps he could work as a dishwasher. Nor could he afford to open his own café in the small Haitian community, which already had a surplus of small sidewalk stands that prepared food for those who could pay something, and often for those who could pay nothing. Like many poor emigrants, the young and physically fit migrated to the citrus groves and vegetable farms where they could always find work . . . at a price.

Carly found Binta in a twelve-bed, ramshackle hospice near Miami in an area known as "Lemon City" where those who had nothing worked in the lemon and orange groves of the wealthy for a pittance. Binta lay under a single sheet on a narrow bed with sagging springs. The screened windows were open to admit a whisper of humid air filled with the pungent odors of horse dung from a nearby livery and rotting mangoes and citrus from stalls situated along the winding dirt road. A cacophony of sounds from the bleak settlement of the grove workers filled the air.

Carly was shocked at the sight of her mother. Binta's black skin had a yellowish cast to it and was drawn like a drum's membrane over her prominent cheekbones. Her once sensuous lips were pulled tight over her sunken mouth exposing her teeth like a broken string of discolored pearls. Under the soiled sheet, her frail body had the shape of a mummy. Carly pulled up a chair and put her face against her mother's and felt the heat from her feverish skin.

"Oh Momma, if I had only known. I would have been here to care for you. Oh Momma, forgive me."

Binta opened her eyes. Seeing the tormented look on her daughter's face, she raised a frail arm and placed it around Carly's neck.

"It was a journey of hope," she said. "It just didn't work out the way Phillipe and I planned."

Binta's breath was coming in quick gasps. She stirred and raised her head and arched her back as if to rise, but fell back, her face grimacing in pain.

"I will always be with you," she said in Creole.

That night, in the privacy of her stepfather Phillipe's squat, three-room cinder block house, Carly pulled a small table into the bedroom to make an altar. She sacrificed the largest animal she could afford to buy, a large rooster, and beseeched the Loa to intercede with the Voodoo god, *Bondye*, to save her mother. But the message Carly received from the Loa foretold something else.

When Binta died during the night, Carly abruptly awoke and felt her presence. She lighted incense coals in a miniature urn, placed it on the altar, and sat with her mother's spirit and prayed. Sometime during the night a stillness settled on the room and Carly fell asleep. When she awoke in the morning, Binta's spirit was gone.

She had waited in vain for the saving word from the Loa. In Voodoo, the will of the Loa was the first and foremost law. They determined the course of everything that happened. A person had to accept the fatalism of the faith or move on to another religion. Carly had always thought that was just the way it was and accepted it. Now for the first time, she began to wonder. Could the rules that govern our lives really be so rigid? Could not a person change the course of her or his life through the power of his own will? What direction in her life would she take from this moment on? As she walked to the window and stared out onto the streets of the small Shantytown and saw the weary, resigned looks on the faces of men, women, and children as they headed to the groves, and as she thought about the futility of their lives, she knew what course she would take. She would remain in Lemon City and take it as her own *hounfo*. She would be the worker's *Mambo*.

Carly moved into one of the run-down, matchbox-like structures thrown together by grove owners to serve as homes for migrant fruit pickers during the season. On a clear day, if she stood tall on the back doorstep, she could see the small cemetery where Binta was buried. The hard, physical labor she had performed while in Gonaives, and the demands on her as a Mambo, had changed Carly's appearance markedly. She had replaced what remained of her body fat with muscle that flexed conspicuously as she worked. Her caramel skin was burnt from exposure until it resembled the deep color of toasted bread. The light freckles around her nose had turned dark. Her generous mouth and lips had tightened into a scar-like pucker on her face. Large hollow brown eyes dominated her face and blazed with fervor. Who was this imposing woman who joined the people on their daily trek to the groves, and could out-work many a man? Who was this who came to them in the middle of the night when they were sick, and gave them council when they were in need? Who, indeed, was she?

One steaming, hot afternoon in the groves where it never seemed to cool off even during the fall "picking" season, a thin black woman approached Carly. Her skin was mottled with large splotches of various pigmentations that gave her the look of recently applied camouflage.

A death-like look of fatigue was on her face. She had only recently come to work, and Carly had not yet spoken with her.

"Miss Carly, mum, when we finish de picking, I needs to talk to you if'n you don' mind," she said, her voice heavy with the accents from the land of cotton in Mississippi, or the fields of to-bacco in the Carolinas.

When the last bag of fruit had been unloaded, the woman, whose name was Jessie, and Carly sat on the wide loading dock, fanning. Jessie was crying.

" Miss Carly, I don' means to bother you none, but I'se heard all 'bout you and I gots no one else to go to. I been bleeding hard even when it's not 'sposed to be my time. De doctors, dey can't keep it stopped. Dey say I can't work no mo, and I don' know how I goin' to take care of my little girl. I needs you try to get me fixed so I can care of us. If'n you can't and I pass, I needs you take over care of my baby. Try to find her daddy. Ain't nobody else 'll do it."

Carly sat quietly thinking about the anguish of this young woman who was slowly hemorrhaging to death. She had been so wrapped up in the faith, she had seldom thought about binding her life to someone and raising a child. But if not her, who? She couldn't bear the thought of seeing any child placed in foster care or an orphanage in this forlorn area. Carly came out of her trance-like state and finally answered.

"Jessie, I'll try to find a way to help you stop bleeding, and I'll talk to the doctors myself," she said with a hopeful smile. But she had been at the hospital and seen her mother dying. Lemon City did not have a physician and depended on whom the grove owners would bring in to the clinic or hospice, usually the least expensive they could find. After all, managing a grove was just a business wasn't it?

After a moment's pause, and a struggle to get the words out, Carly looked Jessie directly in the eye and said, "If anything happens and you are unable to take care of your child, I will take her to live with me as my own, and try to find her daddy."

Jessie sighed and placed her head on Carly's shoulder. Carly slipped her arm around the woman's shoulders and embraced her.

Carly would skip her shift tomorrow and catch the bus to Miami to meet Jessie and go to the hospital. The bus was a shuttle that made two trips a day. One was to pick up day workers who stood at specific locations if they wanted to work that day, and the other to return them at night. Jessie was a day worker. That's all Carly knew. When Jesse did not show up at the selected location, Carly had no way of finding her. Jessie was just another one of an ever-changing flood of people who came to work in the groves. No one remembered her. Carly canvassed the neighborhood but nobody could place her. Carly never saw Jessie again.

On Christmas Eve of 1925 Carly Delome answered a knock on the door of the cabin where she lived in Lemon City. As the door opened and the light from the house flooded the small porch, the cough of an ancient engine was heard as a truck bumped down the dusty road. There in a pool of yellow light stood a small black child of about four years. At her feet was a cardboard suitcase.

"And who might you be?" Carly asked.

The child looked at the floor and shuffled her feet. She wore a red dress and newly polished black patent leather shoes. Her hair was neatly braided into pigtails and tied with red bows. Pinned to her blouse was a small envelope. Carly stooped and removed the envelope and read from the crudely printed note within.

Her name be Olive Mills. Her mama dead. She say bring child to you if she passes.

On a separate worn, yellow slip of paper in a different hand was a scribbled address:

Isaac Mills c/o Harmony Circus
Most times winter in Hanover, North Carolina.

Carly took the child by the hand.
"Come with me now," she said.
Carly led Olive inside. She fed and bathed her and helped her with her pajamas. Then Carly drew her onto her lap in a rocking chair, and began to sing to her an old ballad she herself had heard as a child.

Gilmer White

When Olive's eyes began to close, Carly placed her in her bed and lay down next to her, singing softly:

> He's gone away
> For to stay a little while
>
> And he's coming back
> If he goes 10,000 miles...

PART THREE

A TIME IN BETWEEN

"As love, if love be perfect, casts out fear,
So hate, if hate be perfect, casts out fear."

Merlin and Vivien, Line 41, Alfred, Lord Tennyson

PRIDE AND PASSION

O h, it was *pride* all right, and *passion* too. Lenore Stone couldn't deny any longer that the flower of her youth had begun to fade. Her younger sister Becky was still in high school, and Lenore had already graduated from college and gone to work at the Coastal & Piedmont Railroad for her daddy, the president and CEO. She had been working there for the better part of eight years. All her close friends were married and had children, and here she was, heels clicking on the polished floors of the railroad building, hoping for a real man to come along. Not that she was unattractive either. A little tall and thin for some men maybe, but she had a complexion as smooth and warm looking as sun on water, and iridescent hazel eyes drawn down into a sad clown's face that everyone said was *so* unique; and all this framed by flowing burnished auburn hair that reached almost to her waist. So what in the world was wrong?

Some folks thought Lenore was a little too haughty, but others discounted that and thought it was all about Mr. Rob Thornton, who transferred in from Richmond six years ago to work in the Freight Traffic Department. He was taller than she was with blond hair, blue eyes, and tennis trim. They complemented each other on and off the court. People in Hanover were awaiting the engagement of Miss Lenore Stone and Mr. Rob Thornton when the unthinkable happened! Rob just disappeared one day without a trace. No note. No forwarding address. Nothing. What had caused him to leave, people wanted to know. Had old man Stone uncovered some unsettling revelation in a background check and paid Rob to skip town? Had something abnormal been revealed as their relationship grew that caused Rob to bolt? Whatever it was, Rob was never heard from again, and folks began to wonder about Miss Lenore Stone.

The mystery of what happened to Rob was compounded by a horror movie kind of event concerning a railroad employee named Logan Franks. Some said he and Lenore were getting a little too cozy when young Logan got himself killed in a training event at a switching station in Maaco, North Carolina. The newspaper said his body got caught while he was trying to decouple two box cars, and, well, to spare the gory details, he was decapitated. You can just imagine what that single event did to end the flow of young men showing up at the Stone household. Lenore didn't want most of them anyway. She wanted a real man—one with everything she had missed! Then one day, *the real man* she yearned for came to town.

"Up here from N'awleans," he said. His name was Cyrus Quinn and he was almost seven feet tall, a true hunk of a man. He worked for a dredging company. He said he was the captain of one of the barges the State brought in to dredge the mouth of the Cape Fear River. She met him at a slumming party she and one of her girl friends went to on a dare. She could feel the blush and heat starting to rise in her face when he walked over to introduce himself. His work in the sun had left his skin a dark toast color and his white teeth glistened when he talked. He had long black hair that was drawn back and tied in a ponytail and wore a shirt with the arms cut out that revealed his huge, hard muscles. And his jeans were tight, with the crotch area that couldn't contain what he had down there. She knew from the beginning she had to have him, but how could she work it with her daddy being the kind of son-of a bitch he was.

It turned out she didn't have to. Cyrus had a car, and how would she like to go to Wrightsville Beach on Saturday and dance at a new place called Lumina. That was just the beginning of their secret meetings, but there was a problem. The relationship was getting out of hand. He wanted her to go all the way, and he was *so forceful*, his hands exploring every crevice of her body. She could hardly fend him off. Lenore finally had to tell him she was not the kind of girl maybe he was used to dating in New Orleans, and if they were going to *do those things*, they would have to get married. Then her daddy who seemed to know everything found out what was going on. Gordon Stone was going to have Cyrus run out of town if she didn't stop seeing him. But nobody was going to tell her what to do. She wanted him and he wanted her, so they drove over the state line to Conway, South Carolina, where anybody could get a license and get hitched overnight. They found a justice of the peace and rounded up a couple of witnesses and got married. As soon as they entered the motel room, they started to pull at their clothes and let them lie where they fell. She had never seen a man naked before, and the size of his erect penis startled her, but she went straight for him. She was sore afterwards, but she had one hell of a night.

Cyrus didn't stop to face her family. He headed straight for the barge, so Lenore had to tell them herself. She held back a smug smile as she unfolded the details. She thought her daddy would have a stroke, he was so mad; and her mother had an expression that looked as if someone had farted at the dinner table. How could their daughter marry some transient from New Orleans who worked on a river barge? How could they face their friends at the country club and church? Finally Cyrus came with hat in hand, begging for forgiveness, lying all the way. If he had known who her daddy was, he would have begged him for her hand! Then the strangest thing happened—her daddy hired Cyrus, and to her parent's friends and hers, Lenore was now married to a "railroad man."

It wasn't until after Lenore and Cyrus moved in with her parents that she found out she was pregnant, and what happened afterwards frightened everyone.

LUTHER COMETH

Lenore awoke from the anesthesia and glanced around the room. Her mother stood beside her bed in the recovery room looking at Lenore with pained eyes and a half smile.

"Hi honey," Judith Stone said. "I was worried about you when you didn't wake up right away. You kept talking and crying in your sleep."

A nurse stood by, solid like a weightlifter, her beefy arms crossed over her starched white uniform.

"Momma," Lenore whispered. "How's the baby?"

"It's a boy, honey. He's being cleaned up."

"We'll get you to your bed in a little while," the nurse said. "You'll see your baby there," She stood ramrod straight and looked at the wall.

When they arrived at the private room, the nurse stopped the gurney, and Judith Stone slipped around it and entered the room. After a moment, the nurse wheeled the gurney through the door and transferred Lenore to the bed.

Something was wrong with the scene unfolding before her, Lenore thought. Too many people were crowded into the small room. Her mother took her place on one side of the bed staring across the

95

room at a cheap reproduction painting on the wall. Her kid sister Becky stood on the other, forcing a weak smile. Gordon Stone stood in the corner with the look of a man whose horse had come in last. Lenore's husband, Cyrus, towered at the foot of the bed, his eyes downcast. The nurse from the recovery room had not left, but stood with her arms still folded like a courtroom bailiff forbidding anyone else to enter. It was a scene frozen in time.

As Lenore settled into bed and looked around the room, a sense of foreboding began to well up from some deep place inside.

"Something's wrong here," she said weakly. "Where's my baby? I want my baby."

"Now honey," her mother said, "The baby will be here soon. No need to fret."

Lenore pushed herself up into a sitting position, her eyes fixed on a movement at the door. A middle aged doctor with a black beard laced with white entered the room and stood at the end of the bed facing her. He still had on his white surgical clothing and moved his hands up and down the front as if he were smoothing out wrinkles. He had an uncomfortable look in his eyes.

"Mrs. Quinn, the baby has some abnormalities," he said matter-of-factly. "We wanted to tell you before we brought it in."

Lenore looked at him with a quizzical expression. She sat silently for a moment, then swept the room with wild, fiery eyes.

"Just bring me my damn baby." She cried out.

The first thing Lenore noticed when they handed her the blanket was the weight. It was easily the heaviest newborn she had ever held. It had to weight close to fifteen pounds. When she opened the blanket her eyes became like saucers. A horror scene was unfolding before her. Her mouth dropped open. All that could be heard in the room was the sudden loud intake of her breath.

From within the folds of the blanket, an enormous purple, round face with black eyes emerged with the hard, fixed stare of a jungle cat before it leaps. Its head resembled a casting of a mask that had come out of the mold off center and it sat on an elongated neck that moved towards her as if it were being hoisted on a mechanical lift. It opened its cavernous mouth and began to make a loud sucking sound.

"Sweet Jesus," Lenore murmured as she stared. She finally exposed her breast to him. Luther, as he would be named, was home.

BAYOU TRUTH

L enore was struggling to get Luther to sleep when the knock came. Luther's eyes popped open. Now, damnit, she was going to have to start all over again.

"Mrs. Quinn. It's Captain Dunn from the police. Open up." The voice was insistent.

Lenore came to the door leading a sleepy and fussy Luther by the hand.

She brushed her hair out of her face as she opened the door to face a somewhat florid, medium sized man with black hair combed to the side to cover a bald spot.

"Yes Captain," she said, forcing a smile. "Is something wrong?"

Captain Dunn was holding his hat at his waist and was squeezing it to keep his hands from trembling. He was trying to raise his eyes to meet hers.

"Mrs. Quinn, I hate to tell you this…your parents have been in a serious car accident down on the road to Orton Plantation. They're both in a bad way. The hospital wants you to come right away."

A Time Before the End

They were both dead, of course. Died on already stained gurneys in the emergency room. She had told her daddy about the curve so many times. Now look what had happened!

That's when Lenore's life of privilege, and everything else it seemed, came to an end.

It took a few years to get all the claims ironed out but the first thing that happened was they lost the big house in Forest Hills and, of course, the stable behind it with the two horses. Then followed the lots the family had title to on Masonboro Sound, and all the rest.

It seemed Gordon Stone was heavily invested in speculative stocks and land he hoped one day the railroad would purchase. When the estate sale was concluded and all the bills paid off, there was just enough left for Lenore and her sister Becky, who was coming home with a new baby, to buy a couple of box-like houses in a mixed ethnic neighborhood that folks just called Six Street.

Cyrus hated it. The come down! He hated the day workers in overalls with lunch pails on their way to catch the trolley to work; the smell down here with the train smoke and the paper plant; and, most importantly, he hated the way guys looked at him at work. He didn't sign up for this. He didn't marry a snooty, blueblood bitch to see a car accident wash it all away. That's when he started beating her, and that's when she found out about him.

Luther could hear it coming. The insulation between the walls was practically non-existent. From the place where his Momma sent him, he heard the rumble begin. He crept to the head of the stairs and looked down. Their shadows were on the walls.

"I got something to talk to you about, Cyrus," Lenore said, her voice edged with ice.

Cyrus squared around to face her. His upper arm muscles bulged beneath the skin-tight T-shirt, his thighs flexing visibly under the cotton work-pants. His dark eyes glared at her.

"What's wrong now?" he answered with a groan, running his fingers through his long, black hair.

The tall, thin woman with the narrow face and sad, drawn down, clown eyes angrily pushed her hair to the side.

"You know what's wrong," Lenore said. "All those damn secrets you've been keeping beginning to come out. That's what."

"What the hell you talking about, woman," Cyrus said.

"Things you been keeping from me and everybody else about your life before you came here."

"Ain't nobody else's business."

"Well, it's my business, and I've been hearing some things I don't like at all," Lenore said, raising her voice to a falsetto pitch. "And I got it from good sources...people who know."

"You been checking up on me, huh?" Cyrus said, a sly smile edging its way onto his face.

"Don't make no difference, Cyrus; but sure, I checked up. Took the last of the money my daddy left me to do it. But it was worth it. Found out a lot about you Cyrus. Know you were in jail before you came up here and wormed your way in with my daddy. Almost killed a man with your fists in New Orleans, did you? Been in lots of fights over women, have you Cyrus?"

Cyrus could hear her voice begin to make a hissing sound and slowly backed away.

"But you know that's not the real reason I spent all that money, don't you, Cyrus?"

The repetitive, harsh pronunciation of his name meant it was something really serious. He had heard it before and knew it was just the preliminary to the real fight to come.

There was the sound of sucking wind in Cyrus's throat. "Look, Lenore, I came here to start over. As far as I'm concerned, I left the past behind."

"No, Cyrus, you brought your past with you and kept the truth from me and my family. You knew about your family's secret. Knew what was going on—had been for decades. Knew what the outside world didn't know. Most of all, you knew what was happening to the children."

There wasn't going to be any compromise. Cyrus squared his shoulders and thrust his chin forward like an angry bulldog ready to attack. Might as well face it head on. There was going to be a fight, and fighting was something he knew a lot about.

A Time Before the End

"Yeah, I knew what was happening," he said in a hollow, faraway voice. "Saw my youngest sister get knocked up. Saw my old man coming out of the bedroom and her in there hollering and my momma nowhere in sight. And that's just the start of what I've seen. Saw my brothers do it to whoever they could…white and black, it didn't matter. Seen what the babies looked like that was born ever since I was a kid. You see a lot of that kind of stuff in Bayou country, us being isolated the way we are. Maybe it ain't right with the rest of the world, but that's the way it is down there. Now that you know, I guess you're going to hold it against me. Ain't that right, bitch!"

Lenore stood her ground. Balled up both her fists and held them by her side. "It ceases being about you and me, Cyrus. You could have told me the whole story. About the inbreeding. About the outright incest. About the thing with the negroes. About the idiot children and the deformed ones. About yourself. How you carried the genes. But no, you had to keep it secret and get me pregnant. You knew and still let it happen. And now, look at our son upstairs. Look at Luther. Just look at him and give me another excuse for not telling me, you lying bastard!"

Cyrus laughed. "It ain't my fault he looks the way he does. You didn't seem to care about anything when you first saw me naked and climbed all over me. It was you who birthed a freak, not me."

The muscles in Lenore's face turned as hard as granite, her eyes like a cornered animal of the jungle, fixed on Cyrus's face. She spat on the floor at his feet. She raised her hand to slap him.

"Don't ever call my son that, you dirty lowlife. Don't ever, you hear!"

Cyrus caught her hand in midair and bent it backwards, forcing her to the floor.

Lenore started to scream and Cyrus threw her aside, knocking over a chair. She got slowly to her feet and staggered forward, her arm raised to strike. Cyrus slapped her and pushed her against the wall. Lenore stumbled forward, lost her balance and fell. She cried out, and rose to face him again. The fight went on and on until the house shook. Shadows clashed on the wall as if cast by candlelight in a frightening dark cave.

Luther stood trembling and soaking his pajamas with urine. He knew the beating being inflicted on his momma was because of him, and now he finally knew what was wrong with him.

That night after the cops came to take Cyrus away and Luther got a good look at his momma's severely swollen and bruised face, he thought he heard voices.

A BIRTHDAY PARTY

Luther stood with his back to the door, a birthday gift with a pretty bow in his hands. His mouth was contorted. He was on the verge of crying, dark eyes begging her.

"Momma, they're all younger than me. Please don't make me go. Please!"

Lenore Quinn reached up and pulled his huge head down until she felt the coarse skin against her cheek.

"You've got to go honey," she said softly. "You know Peggy Kinlaw's mom is one of my best friends. And besides, you were invited. It would be very poor manners not to go."

Lenore moved her face until she felt the sandpaper like texture of his lips touching hers. Holding his head gently between her hands, she kissed him softly.

"Go on now," she said. "We'll do something special together when you get home. I promise."

Luther backed out of the door onto the porch silently mouthing the words, "please...please!" Finally he turned and headed down

105

the block and around the corner to little Peggy Kinlaw's house.

It was true most of the kids at the party were younger than Luther, but that wasn't the real reason he didn't want to go. There was something else. Something frightening that happened a week ago, an event that had terrified him, knowing the day of the party would soon be at hand. Now it was here.

As he walked, Luther thought about Peggy Kinlaw and the other girls and boys who would be at the party. He didn't have any trouble with the boys. He could see they were intimidated by his size and looks and enjoyed the power he felt when they moved aside to make a path for him or chose him first for their sports teams. It was the girls who frightened him. He tried to understand why, but couldn't figure it out. He had heard boys at school describe in graphic detail what girls' bodies looked like without their clothes "and there was my big sister there naked in front of the mirror and then she turned around and saw me, golly…" Of course, the closest he could get in his mind's eye to what they were describing were the nude manikins in department store windows. And, because their home was so small, he occasionally snitched a view of his momma in her bra and panties. He wasn't frightened but he certainly didn't feel comfortable around girls, and knew there was a reason for it. Of course, that wasn't a problem most of the time. Girls went out of the way to steer clear of him, giving him a sidelong glance, cupping their hands and whispering.

Little Peggy Kinlaw was different. A thin girl of thirteen with copper colored hair braided into pigtails and luminous, innocent looking green eyes; she didn't seem to notice. That's what he didn't understand. She should be frightened by his grotesque appearance, should be intimidated by his strange behavior; but she wasn't, always looking up at him with guileless, friendly eyes. Even seemed to enjoy talking to him. They were indeed a strange looking pair—the small, stick-shaped girl and the lumbering giant; she with her head bent, looking toward the sky, and he, peering down as if he were an eagle searching for prey. Neighbors laughed at the sight of them walking home from school together. That's how the trouble started. When he looked back on it, what happened that summer on the last day of school was an indelible marker pointing to events to come.

A week before the party, when school finally ground to an end, Luther, who had accumulated an unusual assortment of junk in his locker during the year, finally got it sorted out and stuck what remained in his knapsack. Only the teachers and maintenance crew were left when he hurried out the main entrance and almost ran over Peggy Kinlaw, who had also stayed behind to say a special goodbye to her favorite teacher.

When Peggy looked up and saw Luther, she hesitated momentarily, then smiled and fell in with him, handing him her school bag to carry. It was a dreary, overcast day. Thunder was rumbling in the background. Luther hated to get wet so he persuaded Peggy to take the shortcut. They were hurrying along the narrow path beside the creek, hardly talking, trying to beat the rain. When Luther began to pick up the pace, Peggy started to run to keep up. As she reached him, she stumbled over an exposed cypress root. She said "Oh," and Luther turned to see her sprawling with her arms outstretched. He was wearing his knapsack and carrying hers in his right hand. When he reached out to catch her, he missed her arms. Instead, his left hand snagged her blouse ripping it, tearing it from top to bottom.

Luther quickly got his arm under her armpit, lifting her, and their bodies were suddenly touching. When Luther looked down, he saw the pink, budding nipples of her breasts exposed from beneath the teen bra that had been rudely jerked out-of-place.

Luther was transfixed. To have finally seen a girl's hidden flesh! To have actually touched it as his hand raked across her body! And now to be feeling the soft jutting things pressing against his own flesh. Suddenly, Luther felt a stiffening in his crotch. Hardly realizing what he was doing, he pressed little Peggy Kinlaw's hand against the swelling member rising inside his trousers.

A Time Before the End

For a brief moment, Peggy couldn't comprehend what was happening. When the reality hit her, she jerked her hand away as if she had unknowingly touched a viper.

"Luther . . . What are you doing!" she cried. "*God, what are you doing?*"

She broke loose and started to run, stumbling again.

In a flash Luther went after her. He caught her and pulled her upright. The image of her flesh and the burning he felt with her hand on him took over his mind, eradicating every other thought. He wanted to do what his body was driving him to do.

As he reached down to tear at her remaining clothing, he heard her voice. It sounded like a distant echo.

"Please don't, Luther . . . please," she begged.

Luther's hard black eyes turned to little Peggy's pleading face. A look of terror was in her eyes. He dropped his eyes to her rail-thin body, pink flesh helplessly exposed and unprotected.

In what remained of the small rational window of his mind, Luther realized he couldn't get away with it. His will faltered. He couldn't do it. He let her go.

A groan came from deep within him as he tried to find the words to keep him out of trouble.

"I'm sorry, Peggy," he finally said, his voice breaking. "I didn't mean it. Please don't tell! Please don't! I won't do it again. I promise."

Peggy Kinlaw realized she had the advantage. She covered up her exposed breasts with her arms and faced him. Her pretty face was twisted and red with anger.

"Luther Quinn. How dare you! What were you thinking? You go get my bag right now."

Luther turned and ran. When he brought the bag back from where it had been dropped, she was standing with her back to him, the torn blouse and the bra on the ground at her feet.

"Get my gym sweatshirt out and hand it here," she said, enunciating each word with emphasis. "And don't you dare look!"

Peggy jerked the shirt from his hands and slipped it on. With her hands on her hips she turned to face him. The capillaries in her face were still bristling red.

"You've ruined everything," she cried. "How *could* you do something like that, and how do you expect me to explain *this* to my mother," she said, picking up the torn blouse and shaking it in his face. "And what you did with your hands on me. Do you think I'm going to keep that from her? Why should I anyway?"

Luther stepped back, his lopsided face contorted, his hands outstretched, gesturing wildly, begging.

"Please don't tell, Peggy. My dad will beat me something bad. Think of something to tell your mom. Please."

Peggy looked up at him, her eyes fixed on his. Without saying anything, she turned and ran down the trail toward home, leaving Luther standing in the path, still begging.

Luther stood in the reception line in the Kinlaw's foyer tightly clasping Peggy's birthday present, shuffling his feet, staring at the floor. Beyond the foyer in the large living room a crowd of boys and girls were milling about, some with colorful cardboard hats held on their heads with rubber bands and twirling noise makers in their hands. He was next in line to greet Mrs. Kinlaw and Peggy. Raising his head, he could see their eyes turning toward him.

"What are you doing here?" he imagined Mrs. Kinlaw saying as she turned to her husband, a big beefy guy with a beet red face. "Harold, get this disgusting kid out of here and turn him over to his daddy. Cyrus will take his hide off, that's for sure." And he could almost see Peggy and all the other kids and parents staring at him, mocking him.

"What a dumb thing to do, Luther!"

Luther, head down, extended the present toward Peggy as slowly as if it were a corsage of dead flowers.

"Here... here's your present, Peggy," he said. I...I'm sorry about...

Peggy Kinlaw put her finger to her lips to hush him.

Mrs. Kinlaw placed her hand on Luther's arm and beamed up at him.

"Luther we're proud of the way you protected Peg after school last week. Thought I told your mom. Anyway, we couldn't find the boy who tore her blouse. Probably one of those white trash that have been moving into Castle Street recently."

Little Peggy Kinlaw couldn't hold Luther's hand. It was too large. Instead, she clung to the tips of his fingers. She tilted her pretty head, raised her eyes to his, and winked, and for a long moment kept her eyes fixed on his. When Luther thought about it later, he thought he saw his future foretold in the deep pools of those startling green eyes.

But what a relief! Worried all last week for nothing. Peggy took care of it after all!

Luther hadn't planned to stay at the party, but he could see Peggy's eyes on him, holding him with her secret, and her smile, *owning him now*, daring him to leave before she finally released him.

Luther was worried. He wanted to reach home before his daddy so he could spend time with his Momma. She was waiting for him. But Peggy wasn't going to let him go. He was hers. To be able to manipulate a huge boy like that—what a thrill! When Peggy finally dismissed him, she escorted him to the door with her hand on his arm. An unusually broad, confident smile was on her face.

"Thanks again for coming and staying so long," she said.

As Luther turned to bound down the stairs little Peggy Kinlaw added:

"I can't wait for school to start again. Can you?"

HOMECOMING

lancing back at Peggy Kinlaw's as he walked, Luther could hardly contain himself. She was standing on the porch talking to the mother of one of the partygoers, and he didn't want her to see him running. As soon as he rounded the corner, he bolted for home.

Momma, momma," he yelled as he flung open the front door. "I'm home."

Strange. No answer. She was supposed to be home. That's what she told him. Then he heard the sounds—sobs coming from the downstairs bedroom followed by the convulsive intake of air that sounded like gasps. In a moment the noise abruptly stopped; then it started again—now a forlorn, desolate moan.

Luther rushed down the hall into the room. He had arrived too late. Lenore sat in a straight chair beside the ripped apart covers of the bed, her body upright, back rigid. Her dress was torn from the neck to the waist. One breast was exposed as if she were about to nurse a child... her hairdo a discarded bird's nest. A purple swelling covered her right cheek and neck. Her eyes were swollen, and red from crying. She looked straight ahead.

Luther rushed to her side and put his big meaty arms around her.

"Momma, momma," he cried. "What happened, Momma?"

His voice was the desolate cry of a wounded animal.

Lenore turned to face Luther. Slowly, she reached out and took his distraught face in her hands.

"Something bad happened, Luther. I can't tell you about it now. I need to call your Aunt Becky."

Becky Porter flung the door open and rushed through the house to Lenore's side. Luther had been sent to a room upstairs, but slipped silently down the staircase so he could hear.

"Good God, Lenore. Look what he's done to you! The bastard. He could have killed you. We need to call the police right now!"

Lenore shook her head. She looked hopelessly at Becky.

"You know he's going to say it was just another one of our quarrels that got out of hand. Besides, half the local police get special privileges at that hunting lodge where he guides.

"But he raped you, for God's sake! We're not going to let him get away with it. Forget the damn local police. Him beating you has got to stop. I'm calling the Sheriff's office. Going to talk to Buck Tindal myself. Nobody's going to stand in his way. Buck will bust Cyrus's butt. And don't plan on staying here tonight. You and Luther are spending the night at my house.

Luther had been in his aunt Becky's home many times, but rarely on the second floor where he was now lying awake in a large bed next to his cousin Ben, someone so different acting from himself he felt uncomfortable in his presence. He tried to sleep but couldn't, the voices and images from the evening going round and round in his head. It was midnight when he rose to go to the toilet.

As he felt his way down the dark hall, he passed a room with its door cracked. Pale yellow light found its way into the hall. When he glanced inside, his Momma was standing there nude, unmoving, like a Grecian statue, her nightgown held loosely in one hand, her head bent to the side and downward in a classic pose. A ceiling fan holding a yellow light bulb turned overhead. The flicker of her image came through the door like the action from a silent movie. He could see it all: her sad, ruined face, the black mound between her legs, her large uplifted breasts pointing obliquely away like sentinels on guard, rosette circles surrounding her nipples. Luther found himself aroused. Frightened by his response, he hurried down the hall to the toilet. When he returned, Lenore's door was closed. He stood before it for a moment like a guest seeking entry.

As he sought sleep, Luther tried to blot out the disturbing images from the room, but couldn't forget the portrait of his Momma standing there nude, so beautiful it was too much to bear.

When he awoke later, the house was quiet. They were all asleep except Luther. He lay there in the silence, listening to Ben's breathing, trying to understand everything that was welling up inside him. He thought about little Peggy Kinlaw and the power he felt when he had her in his hands. And about his Momma in that room down the hall and what happened to him. Some force seemed to be taking over his will. It had all begun *here* in Aunt Becky's house, begun in his mind after Miss Carly Delome had entered that room downstairs. What did it mean? Who were the new voices filling his head and talking to him? What was causing the passions driving him?

Now, he felt a new kind of feeling, a blind rage that twisted inside him. One he could not suppress. It was focused on one person—his father, Cyrus. No one was going to hurt his momma and get away with it!

PERFECT HATE

He heard the damn noises again—banging, banging, banging—coming from the room above. Luther lay on the bed listening, flinching with every bang, every thump, every muted groan.

When Lenore came downstairs to make breakfast, Luther confronted her.

"I know what's happening up there," he told her. "I can't stand what he's doing to you. I hear it almost every night now, and it's got so I can't sleep anymore."

Lenore Quinn stepped to the counter to start the coffee. She turned slowly to face him. Her long, narrow face was filled with the hollow look of fatigue. Her eyes were empty of expression, and the puffiness around them told Luther she had been crying.

"Luther, I don't want you to get involved with what's happening upstairs. It's none of your concern."

"Yes, it is Momma. He's hurting you after he said he wouldn't. He's just not doing it with his fists. You got to get help."

Lenore sighed. "I can't do that son. You remember what happened last time, and how long it took our family to get over it."

115

A Time Before the End

Luther hadn't seen what happened himself, but old Tom Jenkins gave everyone who would listen a blow-by-blow description.

"Buck, he done come in the bar asking after Cyrus. Cyrus seen him first, and I guess he knew what was coming. He stood up and broke the end off a beer bottle, and faced ole Buck with it. Now you know Cyrus is pushing seven feet, and Buck is maybe 5'10 if 'un he stands up straight, but none of that slowed ole Buck down. He just unbuckled his holster and handed it to Ed the bartender and went after Cyrus. Cyrus, he jabbed the broken end of the bottle at him, but Buck made a funny sort of a move . . . like this . . . and grabbed his arm. He lifted it up and smashed his hand on the bar, and you could hear it making a kind of crunching sound like it was broke. Cyrus, he screamed, but you know he's strong as a bull, and he grabbed Buck with his other arm . . . like this . . . and they fell against the bar and then down on the floor. Well, when they got back up, you could see ole Buck had lost that patch over his eye, and I tell you, I never seen anything like that before in my whole life. There was this jagged scar and dark hole and ooze where his eye used to be, and everybody was standing there looking at him with their mouths dropped open. I guess Cyrus must,a been too 'cause Buck moved in close and hit him in the stomach and then brought his knee up hard in his balls. Well, Cyrus bent over and grabbed himself, and when he did Buck brought his knee up again smack in his face. I tell you, there was blood and teeth all over the place and Cyrus, he laid there the floor wiggling like a worm doused with kerosene. Well, ole Buck, he dragged Cyrus outside on the sidewalk, and stood straddling him. Told him if he ever hurt Miss Lenore again, or Miss Becky, there wouldn't be any place he could hide. He'd track him down and kill him like a rabid dog and nobody would ever know who done it."

Remembering what Buck said to Cyrus was what gave Luther the idea: "track him down and kill him and nobody would ever know who done it." *The perfect crime.* He had wanted to kill Cyrus after that night three years ago but knew he was too young to do it right without getting caught. Now things were different. He was a lot bigger and stronger, and was thinking better when the voices weren't bothering him. And if his Momma wasn't going to help herself, he'd have to do it for her. He'd known that because of something that happened a few weeks back.

Cyrus was gone for the evening and Lenore wasn't feeling well, so Luther went upstairs to tell her goodnight and found her nude, a sleeping gown on one arm. He had never been able to erase the image of her from three years ago, her perfectly formed nude body poised erect like a Greek goddess as she stood so pensively in that pool of flicking light. Now she stood with her shoulders stooped and her once firm breasts sagging almost to her waist. She had lost weight, and skin hung in loose folds from her waist, thighs, and buttocks. And the purple and yellow bruises he had been seeing on her arms were on her body where they could not be seen when she was dressed. Luther wanted to go inside and pull her close, but instead he turned quickly and walked away. He knew the rage he felt could not be explained. And he couldn't tell Buck Tindal.

Buck would only beat Cyrus again and that wouldn't stop what was happening to his momma. It was up to Luther to stop it. That's when he started to make the plan, and that's when the voices stopped bothering him for a while.

Luther had to catch Cyrus alone where no one was watching so he could get away without being seen or traced. That wasn't going to be easy. There was only one way to get to Cyrus. Luther would have to start spying on him.

Cyrus often caught the trolley home after work, and Luther would hide in storefronts and alleys at stops along the route to see if he was getting off. If Cyrus got off Luther would follow him. But Cyrus always came home when he caught the trolley. Luther could never get to him that way. So what about the other days, the days when Cyrus didn't catch the trolley and Luther didn't see him come out of the train terminal either? Luther was stymied. Then he caught a break. It was late one day and he was about to give up and go home when a sleek Packard pulled up to the terminal entrance. A lady with platinum blond hair was driving, and the moment she pulled up under the roof, Cyrus ran out and jumped in. They both leaned over and kissed, and she quickly drove off. That's when Luther knew what was going on, but he had to find out where Cyrus was going with the woman with the silver hair.

Luther decided to ride his bicycle after school, or on lazy summer days when school was out, looking for the silver Packard. That's when he got another break. It was late on a Friday afternoon when Luther turned the corner of Sixth Street onto Castle and was headed north when he saw the silver Packard parked in front of the liquor store. He quickly pulled into an alleyway, ran to the edge of a building and peered around the corner. There was his daddy coming out of the liquor store with a large box. Then he went back inside and brought out another one. Funny, today was Friday, and recently Cyrus wasn't coming home on Friday or Saturday night. Always told Lenore he had a hunting or fishing party early the next morning at the lodge he managed for the railroad executives.

Luther edged around the corner and hid behind a row of trashcans at the next building. Now he could see the silver haired lady in the driver's seat and Cyrus beside her. Before he knew it, the car was gone.

Two doors down from the liquor store was a hardware store. Luther ran and entered the store. An old man with red capillaries in his cheeks dipping snuff stood at the counter.

"Do you know who owns the silver Packard that comes through here?" Luther asked, breathlessly.

"I ain't seen you before around here," the man said, taking a swipe with the back of his hand across his mouth to wipe away the juice. "Why you want to know, boy?

Luther thought the truth might be the best answer.

"Live over on Sixth Street. My daddy's supposed to be with my momma, and we got an emergency. I need to find him."

The old man cleared his throat. It was difficult talking to a kid about things like this

"Well son, I guess your daddy's a lucky man. That'd be Miss Faye. She owns a house about a mile out of town that entertains men, if you know what I mean. Keep on this road to you hit the city limits. Ain't far beyond that. Set back in the woods. You'll find it if you look for the road with the red mailbox on the highway. That's how guys who ain't been there before find their way."

Luther was getting tired but kept on peddling until he found the red mailbox. He hid his bike in a ditch then took to the woods along the dirt road so he wouldn't be seen. He ended up at a big rust colored house. It looked like an ordinary two story country home with a veranda on three sides and baskets of ferns and flowers hanging from the ceiling up over the railings. To a stranger journeying down the dirt road, it was just a sleepy country residence with probably an old couple inside drinking hot tea before they retired for the evening.

Luther wanted to find the other entrances to the house and moved through a circle in the woods. In the rear there was a parking area with four cars. Among them was the silver Packard. There were rear doors at both levels of the house with a flight of wooden stairs leading down to the parking lot. Luther figured the setup was designed so guys could come and go without being seen from the front driveway.

Luther was still trying to work out his plan to get to Cyrus when the downstairs rear door flung open and Cyrus walked out to the Packard and started looking around the parking lot.

Luther panicked. God, had the guy from the hardware store called Miss Faye?

But Cyrus just took a deep breath of fresh air and stuck his head in the trunk and came out with a case of what looked like whiskey and carried it into the house. He hadn't been more than twenty yards from where Luther stood in the woods. Too close to

119

call, but now he had his plan. Today was Friday. They bought liquor on Friday, and his daddy probably did most of the buying. If he didn't come home Friday evening, Luther knew from Cyrus's habits he was probably going to stay the weekend. The question was would there be a time when he would be in the house alone or with the woman named Faye. Sure wouldn't be Friday or Saturday. That's when this place would be seeing action until the wee hours. No two ways about it. He was going to have to come back Sunday morning. That's the only time Luther was going to catch Cyrus alone—when everyone else had cleared out—and he'd still be lucky to pull it off without being seen. Didn't make any difference. Luther was going to do it anyway.

FATE PLAYS
A HAND

The key was the weapon. It had to be deadly at close range. He couldn't just afford to wound him. Luther went to his daddy's gun cabinet and chose a Winchester double barrel 12-gauge shotgun. He wouldn't remove it yet because Cyrus might still come home and check. He did that all the time if he was planning to guide a hunt the next day. But Cyrus didn't come home Friday night or even by midnight Saturday night. Luther knew it was time to act. His momma was taking sleeping pills now, and she wouldn't wake up until late morning. He'd be home before then.

Luther took the shotgun to the outside shed where Cyrus had a workbench. He snapped down the forearm and released the barrel from the stock. He placed the twenty-eight-inch barrel in a vice. He decided to cut it off at sixteen because it would fit better in his backpack. Just as important, the choke on the barrel would be removed by the cut to leave an open bore close combat type weapon. He took a hacksaw and cut off the excess length of the barrel. Luther removed eight double-aught shotgun shells from a box and put the gun's stock, barrel, and shells in his backpack, and on top placed a sandwich he had made for himself, and a small canteen. He heard the faint clang of the grandfather clock from inside the house. It was midnight. The moment had finally come. He was ready.

Luther was good with a bike. He rode fast despite his size, keeping to the sidewalks and alleys, reversing himself quickly if he spotted someone out for a walk. This was a tough neighborhood. There wouldn't be too many folks out for a stroll this time of the morning. With his black clothing and face paint, no one was going to identify him anyway.

Where Castle Street made a junction with the road that led to the red mailbox, Luther came to a field where a giant "antique sale" was held on weekends. It was always scattered with junk nobody wanted to cart home, and that's where Luther ditched his bike after wiping it down for prints. It would be gone before morning and somebody else's prints would be on it. He would hike the rest of the way.

Luther kept off the highway skirting the edge of the woods. When he saw headlights, he stepped into the shadows of the trees. When he arrived at the house on the lane with the red mailbox, he took a position at the place he had stood before, in the cover of the woods behind the house. It had to be close to 3 AM. Cars were still in the lot. It was obviously a busy night. Four o'clock came. The Packard and two other cars were left. Time was beginning to squeeze Luther. Dawn would come early, and he had to be long gone before the cleaning crew arrived. Five o'clock! Luther was preparing to leave, when two pretty, young women and a man came out laughing, climbed into the cars, and left. Only the silver Packard was left.

Finally, he could do it! Luther assembled the shotgun, opened the breach and inserted two of the eight buckshot shells. He slipped into his backpack and walked toward the house. He reached the entrance to the ground floor and slowly turned the handle. It was locked! With all the people coming and going, he hadn't thought about the door being locked. What was he going to do? Luther decided to try the door on the second floor up the steps. When his hand twisted the doorknob, the door creaked open. Immediately, he was hit by the smells of the evening: cigarette and cigar smoke mixed with the odor of human exertion, compounded by the smells of deodorants and whiskey.

"They won't be up here," Luther thought. "Not with this smell."

He went slowly down the stairs, placing his feet softly on the carpet. The entrance to the house was on his right and the parlor straight ahead where you sat until the girl of your choice came to get you. There was another room with chairs and two love seats where you got to size up the girls if you didn't already have a favorite. Then there was a kitchen and finally a rear bedroom down a short hall. All the lights were off except a low wattage light in the kitchen and one in the hall.

Luther knew Cyrus and the pretty silver-haired Faye were behind the door in that bedroom. He didn't want to hurt her, but if he backed off now it would be his momma who got hurt.

Luther slipped the shotgun's safety off and walked straight to the door. He flung it open. The light from the hall fell upon the bed where Cyrus and Faye were sleeping. A fan turned slowly overhead.

"Cyrus, Luther cried out.

Faye rolled over on her back and pushed herself up to look at Luther. She was nude and her breasts, like her face, were immediately drawn taut.

"Oh, my God," she said.

Cyrus jerked himself up and sat erect. His hair on his chest was matted and beaded with sweat.

"Luther, what're you doing here boy?" he said, his voice trembling.

Luther shot them both. The sound of the shotgun echoed throughout the empty house.

Then Luther reloaded the gun and shot them again.

Luther took a last look at the devastation lying before him, then stooped to pick up the ejected shell casings and slowly closed the door behind him. His momma was safe at last!

The night had retreated and the morning was creeping in when Luther reached the swamp. He had come this way on purpose.

A Time Before the End

Luther had found the hidden path by accident. He knew a creek ran through the city, joined some other tributaries, and emptied into the Cape Fear River. One day he decided to follow the creek towards its source as far as he could. As he hiked along its banks, the creek made a sharp swing to the right and passed through a swamp shielded by Cyprus and filled with dead trees that had flourished on dry land in the distant past. Luther couldn't figure out how he could go any further until he found a path that skirted the edge of the swamp.

That's where he was now, on the edge of the swamp about to join up with the creek again. Then he would follow it until he was roughly parallel to his part of town. That's where he would leave the creek and reach home by back alleys without being seen. All he had to do now was walk into the swamp until it sucked at your feet, submerge the shotgun and remaining shells, and walk out. The swamp was like a giant octopus. It sucked everything into its maw, and whatever the object was, it was gone. He was almost home free.

Luther dropped his backpack on the path and removed the stock, forearm and barrel of the shotgun. He fitted the parts together He needed the weight of the barrel to hold the other pieces down. He stepped toward the swamp.

"Hi, Mister Luther," a voice echoed in the stillness of the morning. "What you doing with that gun. Ain't nothing to shoot down here."

Luther swung around, the gun pointed forward, slowly reaching for the remaining shells in his pocket.

"Oh, hi Yolinda… it's you," Luther said. "Sort of early for you to be up, ain't it?"

"I likes to come down here early on Sunday when my daddy lets me."

Yolinda was the big retarded black girl that lived close by where the neighborhoods started downhill towards the river. He had seen her often in this part of town, usually in the overrun lots where blacks and whites sometimes played together. She was pretty for a black girl, he thought. All except for the empty faraway look in her large, brown eyes. But the boobs! He hadn't seen white girls with tits like that. Every time he saw her, he thought about it . . .

Luther pushed the lever sideways and pulled the barrel down. The breech opened.

"See Yolinda, the barrels are empty," he said. "I can show you how the gun works if you'd like to see."

Yolinda looked happy to see the gun was empty. She walked over, her large breasts swinging side to side, her pretty innocent face untroubled.

"Here Yolinda, You hold the gun. Let me get behind you and show you. That's easier.

Luther slipped behind and reached his arms around her.

"OK Yolinda, see these shells. You put them in the gun like this…"

"Mister Luther! You're touching me in the wrong places. You got to stop that! Mister Luther, you're hurting me too. Please, Mr. Luther."

Yolinda began to cry.

SEARCHING FOR YOLINDA

L etting the wind at his back push him along, fifteen-year-old Benjamin Porter began to pick up the pace. Only two more blocks before he turned the corner and saw the old two-story wood framed house where he lived. On his back, a knapsack held the last remains of the school year—rumpled blue books, No. 2 pencils with broken lead, erasers, and an assortment of just plain junk. Following a call from the school's custodian, he had finally cleared out his locker. As he stopped briefly to balance the load, he turned his attention to the growl of thunder in the distance. The rank smell of rain was in the air. The summer storm would catch him if he didn't hurry.

Without a word of warning, a young girl stepped from behind a hedge and blocked his path. Ben skidded to a halt.

"Hi, white boy," she said with an impish smile.

"Hi yourself, Olive," he said. "You almost got run down."

"I knoooow," she said, stretching out the word.

"Well, whatcha doing here?" Ben asked.

"Miss Carly sent me with a message for you, white boy." She pursed her lips into a little pout that turned into a grin. Devilish dark eyes seemed to mock and taunt him.

"You know my name!" Ben said, pushing his face close to hers.

"But I allllways call you 'white boy,'" Olive said, bending forward with hands on hips in a mock gesture of defiance.

The late summer humidity had begun to cover the city in a blanket. When the rains came, steam would rise from the sidewalks, plants would droop, and dogs would lie panting. The 'dog days' had already gotten to Olive. She wore a plain, thin, cotton dress that was glued to her body by the moisture. Her long legs rose to a high waist that immediately gave way to the youthful, jutting breasts of a young girl, breasts that already had begun to fulfill the promise of what would come. Her expressive black face was the setting for eyes of ebony and lips that pulled back from a full mouth to reveal the startling white of perfectly aligned teeth. She had a straight nose with a flair at the nostrils, and her face was framed by coal black hair that was drawn back and tied by a red ribbon.

"Well, whats Miss Carly want?" Ben pressed her, trying to keep his eyes off the shape of the body almost pressing against his.

Olive shook a finger at Ben as if she were admonishing a small child. "Don't hand me that stuff. You know what she wants, Ben Porter. She wants you to help search for Yolinda. *Everybody know* Yolinda's been missing since Luther's daddy got killed. They say it happened all within a few of miles of each other. Miss Carly, she think the two things connected. She wants you to help find her. That's what!"

Ben frowned. He wasn't looking forward to searching for anybody in this weather. "Tell Miss Carly I'll join in with the search after I do some chores for my mom."

Olive's dark eyes opened so wide Ben could see the whites. "That what you gwine do, white boy," Olive said, mimicking a black shanty town dialect and sticking her face nose to nose with his. "You say you gwine do it when you gets good and ready. Is that it? That's what you wants me to tell Miss Carly, white boy?"

Ben stepped back. Olive was something else when she got her back up. "O-Kay, O-Kay. I'll stop by Miss Carly's soon as I drop my books off. If I get in trouble, Miss Carly will have to explain it to Mom."

Olive gave Ben a quick intimate smile, made a graceful pirouette and turned to leave.

"See you at Miss Carly's in an hour," she said.

Someone once asked Miss Carly Delome, "What is it about those two that make them seem like brother and sister, or, God forbid . . . ?"

Miss Carly angrily brushed off the question, but in her heart she knew the answer. She had seen it early in their relationship beginning on that stormy night when Becky Porter took Carly and Olive, wet and cold, into her home and fed and clothed the two strangers she knew only as beggars. It became apparent almost from the beginning that Ben and Olive shared a kind of innocent intimacy that few children ever knew. It was as if there was an almost invisible membrane that separated the hearts of the two and what one heart knew, the other knew as well.

Suddenly, one summer afternoon, the innocence of childhood ended. Kids were playing at a creek where a thick vine had been cut loose from the bottom so that those who dared could swing across the creek, turn, and swing back. Olive was in the middle of her swing when the vine broke. She crashed into the water and the shallow creek bed beneath. She lay stunned, rolling over and over with the flow of the water. Ben was watching and without a thought leaped into the water after her. The water was moving swiftly and Olive was still bobbing up and down when Ben reached and wrapped his arms around her. She pulled herself into his arms and continued to let him hold her, and he felt the full imprint of her wet body against his. They continued to cling to each other pressing their bodies together. Finally, gasping, Olive pushed herself away.

"We can't do this," she said.

129

Miss Carly sat at the table in her spirit room, her head bent, seemingly deep in thought. Slowly she raised her head and looked at Olive, Ben, and Black James who had just entered the room. "Search party's about to give up," she said. "Nobody seems much interested in a big ole retarded Negro girl, so it's up to us to find Yolinda. James, you worked on all these back roads in your day. I know you're tired, but you got to search on. Ben and Olive, I need you two to walk the creek about two miles. She's not likely to have gone further than that, her daddy says. And he's already looked, but you never know."

Cooper' Creek ran southeast toward the Cape Fear River Basin until it passed through Hanover. It flowed down the incline through the swale of the Basin slicing its way through thick woods and fragrant flower-filled vales until it merged with a larger tributary that carried it all the way to the big river itself.

Ben and Olive followed its route as it made its way less than a mile from where Yolinda lived. Soon it would enter the swamp where their search would end.

"I guess this is where we need to turn back," Olive said, motioning to the impasse ahead. I know Miss Carly don't want us to wade through that snake infested swamp."

"Yeh, I guess. But if somebody wanted to get rid of a body, wouldn't this be the place. Let's push on a little farther." Ben said.

The shadows from the dark entry to the swamp reached out to enfold them as they descended into the brown cypress-stained water. While it was shallow there, it was tough to see beneath the murky water as they forged ahead toward where the deep water of the creek lay hidden beneath mounds of swamp plants. Holding Olive's hand, Ben led her further and further into the mouth of the swamp until the late afternoon light began to fade. Each dark shape before them became alive with the menace of the approaching night. If Yolinda's body was here, where would it be hidden?

"Ben, I'm getting scared," Olive said. "We don't have a flashlight or anything, and I can't tell which way we came in. We need to start back now."

Ben turned to point behind him.

"OK, I know we go back that way. Even if we're off course a little bit, we'll run into those telephone poles you see on the edge."

They started back, hand in hand, careful to avoid the creek bank. Everything was beginning to look the same when they spotted the dead, hollow trunk of an oak tree on a hummock, a small wooded island of dry land rising from the swamp. It had been easy to miss when they entered, sitting to their left hidden by swamp growth.

As Ben and Olive approached the hummock they heard the noise—a high-pitched buzzing sounding as if it were coming from the very bowels of the swamp itself.

"Ben, I'm telling you," Olive said, tugging on his hand, "I'm gettin' scared. Let's get out of here now."

"Wait a minute, "Ben said. "You know what that sounds like?"

"I don't care, Ben. Let's go."

Every once in a while Ben would surprise himself with a show of bravado that was completely uncharacteristic of his reticent nature. "No, I got to look," he said.

Ben stepped off the bank and waded toward the hummock, the murky water rising to his waist.

Frustrated at his defiance, Olive crept along behind him.

Pushing aside the foliage, Ben inched to where he could clearly see the tree. "Olive, Olive. It's what I thought. It's bees! Come look!"

Bees were buzzing in and out of a huge hole in the trunk of the base of the tree.

"Olive, I bet they've got a hive and are making honey."

Olive moved up beside him. Side by side crept closer. The bees seemed to sense their presence and became agitated. The noise increased. Bees tumbled out of the dark hole, circling the tree, guarding their treasure.

"White boy, we're gonna get stung," Olive said, her voice trembling.

Ben pointed to the ground in front of the tree.

"Look Olive! Look at those marks on the ground where the brush has been beat down. Could be a bear's been here looking for honey. They got some around here, you know."

"But what's that smell?" she said. It don't smell like honey to me. Oh my God, Ben, something's dead in there!

"I'm gonna try'n get close enough to see," he said.

"You're gonna get eat up by those bees," Olive said. "Let's go get the sheriff."

"I got this idea. Read about a guy who did it. I'm gonna try it first."

Ben walked off the hummock into the swamp. He thrust both hands under the water and with a sucking sound brought up two handfuls of sticky black muck. He closed his eyes and spread it on his face and the top of his head. Then he repeated the procedure until the muck covered all of his exposed flesh. When he had finished, he walked out of the water toward the big cavity in the tree. The bees began to swarm and light on him. Still he moved forward until he stood facing the black orifice in the tree. Now the black slime on his body was covered with bees. Olive screamed. He fanned the air in front of him.

"OK, here goes," he said. With a sudden forward movement, Ben thrust his head into the maelstrom storming toward him from the tree trunk.

His shout echoed from the hollow of the tree like a muted clap of thunder.

"Oh God! Oh God!" he yelled as he pulled his head from the tree.

"What is it Ben? What is it?" Olive cried.

Ben bent over and began to heave.

"It's Yolinda," he sputtered. "She's naked, and the bees are covering her body."

HASTE MAKES WASTE

The story spread through Hanover like wildfire. Everyone was laying the blame on Luther. A sheriff's deputy told the story to the crowd who stood in a circle around him:

"Yep, I was there with Sheriff Tindal through the whole thing. We think we got it figured out—got Luther dead to rights. Some Boy Scouts exploring down the creek found the shotgun we think Luther used to shoot his daddy. I guess he thought he had it hid. Belonged to old Cyrus and had Luther's fingerprints on it. The Negro girl, what's her name? Yolinda? She musta seen him with it. Old George, the coroner, he said she was raped and mutilated, the way he put it. Course, I can't go into all the details with the trial coming up, but I'll tell you, he had honeybee bites all over his face and hands. Told everybody he just stumbled into a beehive. That's what he said. I ain't never been involved in a case like this before, and I hope I won't ever be again. Seeing her pulled out of the tree trunk and laid on the ground like that with all the world to see turned my stomach, and I told Ellen, my wife, don't you fix me no dinner anytime soon; and, heh, heh, my Ellen, she says, I don't need to eat dinner no way. You think you know people, like I've knowed Luther since he was a little kid, but then maybe you never do."

The trial lasted two days. When they convicted Luther of the First Degree Murders of Cyrus, Faye and Yolinda, Luther's aunt, Becky Porter pleaded with the jury not to sentence him to death because of his mother Lenore's frail physical and emotional health, and because of his youth. As the deputies led Luther out in chains, Lenore, who had mustered the strength to come to the sentencing, reached over the rail to touch him, and then collapsed. Luther strained to reach her but the deputies pulled him along. As they reached the exit to the courtroom, Luther suddenly set his feet and twisted to face Ben and Olive.

"I know what you did," he shouted. "If I ever get out, I'll kill you. You hear, I'll kill you both!"

PART FOUR

INTERLUDE

A LOVE STORY

As shadows cast by the setting sun crept through the Venetian blinds onto Becky Porter's face, they caused her to raise her head and steal a glance at the man sitting next to her holding the tangled ball of yarn. Despite her normal reserve when she was around him she had to smile. It was just so ridiculous. A man as tough as it gets cradling the jumbled mess in his lap as gently as if it were a newborn kitten. Despite his damaged face and the years that had passed, in her heart he was still the boy she had fallen in love with. But that was before everything happened and her life changed.

Sheriff Hubert Jackson Tindal, called by his nickname Buck by everyone except the criminals who had the misfortune to fall into his hands, sat in the parlor of Becky's home fingering the needles and the yarn that were supposed to produce an Argyle sock. As Buck bent closer to inspect his work, he scowled. Something was definitely not right. He turned towards Becky who was sitting beside him opposite his eye with the black pirate's patch.

"Darn it, B ... B ... Becky," Buck stammered. "I just can't get this what-you-call-it stitch right. How many times we ever gonna use it anyway?"

She almost laughed. She knew he only stammered around her. "Now Buck," Becky said with a quick smile that expressed far less than what she felt, "You know Ella Johnson volunteered to teach knitting to the group, and we all said 'Yes.' I believe you're still a member of the group, *aren't you?*" The last line was delivered in that tone of voice school teachers sometimes use to admonish smart-alecky students, but Becky did not resemble any teacher who ever taught Buck. At fifty-three she still had the figure of a younger woman with smooth skin and liquid indigo-blue eyes that reminded Buck of an undulating wave of flowers he had once seen in a field in France.

"Yeah, I'm still a member, but I don't understand why," he said somewhat gruffly. But, of course, deep within, he understood. So did she. Both were trapped by the past and couldn't forget what had happened. Only, there was part of the memory that belonged to Becky alone, a piece Buck didn't have. It was a secret she had held in her heart, only she had kept the knowledge to herself so long she had begun to doubt its truth. Did it really ever exist?

The frown on Buck's face finally broke into a crooked smile, and like a small child he mischievously pushed the tangled snarl of knitting towards Becky; but her eyes had shifted across the room where a woman with a vacant stare sat rocking back and forth picking invisible specks from the empty space around her.

"He's coming, isn't he?" Becky whispered as if she were talking to no one in particular.

Buck turned to look at Becky's older sister Lenore, who, becoming aware of the attention was now rocking faster and pulling at her hair.

"Yep, he's coming. For sure. Told everybody he was. Already killed that guard trying to get here. You don't think anything or anybody's going to keep Luther from trying to see his momma over there, do you?" he said with a nudge of his chin toward Lenore.

Becky shuddered. "Maybe we should move her to someplace safer," she said.

"Unless you put her in the asylum at Dix Hill, one place is as good as another.

Becky started to cry. "I can't let her go, Buck. I just can't."

Buck took Becky's hand in his.

"I know you can't, but I got deputies watching the house, and I'll be close by to help you all I can."

"Becky managed a smile.

"Thank you, Buck dear," she said.

Most everybody living in Hanover, North Carolina, both white and black, had heard the rumors about Becky Porter and Buck Tindal. Rumors going back more than thirty years. People still talked about them when they didn't have anything else to talk about, but when Buck started showing up at Miss Becky's for knitting lessons, well, tongues began to wag again like it had all happened just yesterday. Older folk, those still around, said there had been a fairy tale romance between the two—the stunning, beautiful daughter of the richest family in town and the backwoods county sheriff's ruffian son. Then something bad happened to change things, and Buck left to fight in World War I. And Miss Becky, well, she went off to college and got herself pregnant while Buck was still recuperating from wounds in a hospital in France. She came dragging herself home a few years later with a baby on her hip but no husband although some said there were papers showing she had been married and divorced. Nobody could prove otherwise, but nobody cared much about proving stuff like that back then. However, as folks began to imagine what was happening at Miss Becky's during those "knitting lessons," well, they just wanted to make sense of it all. The funny thing was, so did Buck.

She was the daughter of Gordon Stone, the urbane Coastal & Piedmont Railroad boss, and his wife Judith, a pillar of Hanover society and its social maven. Buck was the youngest of the five sons and two daughters of Hiram Tindal, the skinny, underpaid, always scrounging local sheriff and his strong-willed, over sized, bonnet-and apron-wearing wife, Jessie, a tough woman in the pioneer mold if there ever was one.

A Time Before the End

The Tindal family lived off a hard packed dirt road in a low lying part of the county loosely called "Dry Pond," with the closest house almost a mile away. They liked it that way. They had a garden, chickens, a few hogs and a milk cow, and the boys could hunt for game. All the while, Jessie Tindal raised her brood with a firm hand. Few could fathom the nature of the relationship between the easily politically intimidated, scrawny Hiram and the determined, no nonsense mammoth-sized Jessie, but it couldn't be any stranger than the one between Becky and Buck, who never would have found each other if it hadn't been for an unusual meeting between their fathers.

One autumn evening, at dusk, when the older boys were away, and Hiram and Buck were sitting on the front porch of the family-built pioneer-style farm house, a black Pierce Arrow "66" roared down the road, raising dust and filling the air with the noise from its high-powered engine. The car came to a sliding stop in the yard before them. After a moment's hesitation, Gordon Stone, dressed in brown corduroy slacks and a short, black leather jacket, stepped out and straightened his tall frame. Under the coat, a white shirt was open at the throat and the black hair from his chest stood out in contrast. He walked to the front steps and stood on the trampled ground before it. Without speaking, Hiram rose and descended the steps to meet him.

"Buck, you step away until Mister Stone and me get through talking," Hiram said.

Buck jumped down and walked out to the car.

He stood for a moment admiring its form and glossy finish. He circled the car to get a better angle. When he reached the passenger door, he saw Becky Stone looking at him through the open window.

Color rushed to his face. It burned hot. Before him sat the girl whose unusual beauty and haunting presence had always left him tongue-tied, gawking, frozen in place. The girl who lived up the hill in a neighborhood protected by swinging gates in a part of town where he wasn't welcome. He was looking directly at her, his face less than a yard away. Under a swirl of strawberry blond hair, unblinking indigo-blue eyes stared back at him from the recessed cover of her brows like an animal's eyes from a dark cave. What were they saying to him? Were they angry he had intruded? And what did the mischievous twist of her full, unpainted red lips mean? Buck was struck dumb.

"Well, Buck Tindal, are you finally going to speak to me after all this time?" Becky said.

Buck dropped his eyes. He tried to calm his mouth. "Huh . . . hi . . . Buh . . . Becky," he said. "What're ya . . . ya . . . you doing here?"

"I asked Daddy to bring me. I've never been out this way before."

Buck knew he had to change the subject if he was going to keep his stammering under control. "I seen you with the other cheerleaders," he said.

"We're practicing for football season. I saw you win the wrestling."

"It . . . it was a hard match."

"But you won, Buck. You won!"

"I'm glad you saw it," he said, finally raising his head.

Her unyielding eyes continued to linger on his, her hand resting tantalizingly on the side of the door. He wanted to reach out and do what he had yearned to do for so long—to finally touch her. Suddenly he heard the driver's side door slam. Gordon Stone had slipped into the driver's seat. The electric starter began to whine and the car started. He backed up and turned. Becky waved. The mysterious eyes disappeared. She was gone.

Buck stood for a moment waving, looking at the cloud of retreating dust. When he turned toward the house, he saw Hiram standing on the porch with a white envelope in his hand.

Buck has stopped knitting. He is trying to retrieve something lingering below the surface of his memory. The room seems frozen.

Nothing is moving. Becky sits beside him, her knitting resting in her lap. Across the room, her sister Lenore has stopped picking invisible specks from the air.

Suddenly, the absurdity of it hits him. He, Buck Tindal, the tough, no-nonsense county sheriff, sitting in a parlor in the stillness of the late afternoon, still stammering in the presence of the woman who broke his heart so many years ago, while across the room a deranged woman rocks to an unknown cadence. Buck Tindal, a grown man, acting like a fool: a love-sick, callow youth, wanting to make things right when he doesn't even know what has gone wrong; trying to fit the pieces of a scattered picture puzzle together, only to find the center piece is missing and he can't find it.

The romance became full blown the summer following high school graduation after the seemingly impenetrable barrier between Buck and Becky had been broken. He was working in town lugging crates at the Coca-Cola Bottling Company. He worked in the summer heat with his shirt off. His barrel chest was tanned the color of polished leather and his blond hair bleached from the exposure to the sun. She came upon him there. She was standing outside the ring of the workers, looking in. When they saw her, they turned and stared. They could not see her legs for the long skirt, but her arms were bare under the summer blouse, and her full breasts pressed against the light fabric.

When the workers went on break, Buck pulled on a t-shirt and walked over and stood facing her.

"I came this way to the cemetery to see my family's plot," she said. "When I saw you, I thought you might want to go with me. It's sort of scary over there."

She led him two blocks to a brick wall with an iron gate. She had a key to the huge lock, and they pushed open the rusted gates and stood inside. The sun glistened on their skins. Silence was everywhere.

"They're buried at the back," she said. "We're one of the oldest families in this cemetery. My something-great grandfather on my father's side, Thomas Stone, was a sea captain. His ship went down off the Outer Banks. He had one son. That's where we came from. My mother's family, the Beerys, came from Knotts Island, North Carolina, and settled along the Cape Fear River to build ships. They're all here. I like to come here sometimes and just be silent and wait. Sometimes I think they speak to me. I hope you don't mind if I share all this with you."

"No, I . . . I don't B . . . Becky," he said. "I wish I . . . I knew where all my kin were buried."

She turned and looked him directly in the face, her deep-set, fathomless eyes, fixed on his. She took his head with the damp, blond curls in her hands and kissed him hard on the mouth, her body pressing against him. She felt him trying to respond, and she kissed him again, this time letting her moist lips and tongue move over the surface of his lips. "This is to teach you, Buck Tindal, you don't have to stutter around me," she said softly.

He stood for a moment, his arms wrapped around her, breathing in her perfume and the earthy essence of her; and time stood still for Buck.

When he finally spoke, it was in a voice he did not recognize.

"Darn it Becky. You've gone and ruined me for anybody else."

There was born on that afternoon an indefinable, hopeful feeling about their future that only the furtive, doomed summer relationships of graduating high school seniors could nourish. She would go off to college in Raleigh, and he would apply for an appointment to the police academy there, and then they would be able to be with each other without having to sneak around. Could anything so real and unsoiled be brought to an end?

It was brutally hot, that windless summer in 1916. Clusters of drooping Wisteria hung from trees, and the pungent smell of

Magnolias and honeysuckle clung to the humid air. Becky and Buck tried to keep what they had together alive. They met again in the cemetery at first, but her parents suspected something, and then she couldn't get away anymore. After that, she worked out a scheme with girlfriends, whose parents had summer cottages at the beach, to meet for sleepovers. She would walk on the beach with her friends, and then slip away to meet Buck, and they would lie hidden in the sand dunes among the sea oats.

Hiram Tindal had risen to his position by being suspicious of everyone and using what he discovered as currency to get ahead. When he found out about Buck and Becky, he was terrified. He was appointed rather than elected. His job, everything he had, depended on what he was able to pass on to those in power. If Gordon Stone found out about his daughter and Buck from someone else, Hiram would be on the outside looking in. There were plenty of others who wanted his job. When Hiram left the spacious mahogany appointed office of Gordon Stone, Becky was abruptly grounded. No daughter of the Stones was going to sneak around with the grubby son of an on-the-take sheriff!

Suddenly, she was whisked away on a family vacation to their summer place at Grandfather Mountain. When the family returned to Hanover, it was just in time to gather Becky's things and leave for Raleigh where she was enrolled in Peace College, her mother's alma mater, a school exclusively for young women. Judith Stone sat down with her friend, the Dean, and explained the situation.

"Catherine, she's gotten herself involved with a boy she can never marry, and Gordon and I want it to end. Frankly, we need your help in watching her until this unfortunate mess blows over."

Catherine Carter snorted. She was tall and lean with the knowing look of someone who had seen it all and dealt personally with most of it.

"Come on Judith," she chuckled. "You know what a bitch I can be when I set my mind to it. When I get finished, even you are going to have a hard time getting to see your daughter."

Carmen McKenna was a fiery redhead radical and the senior class rebel. She sat on a low concrete wall with her legs crossed and her skirt hiked up over her knees. She was smoking a Chesterfield cigarette and blowing smoke from the pucker of her crimson painted lips. She was looking down at Buck who stood on the ground in front of her.

"Old lady Carter is a real bitch, all right," she said. "I didn't last a month at Peace, and boy, are my mom and dad pissed off. They say they're going to send me to a 'miss somebodies' school up North where I can't get out. But look, Buck, ain't no way you're going to see Becky anytime soon. You know her old man."

Buck's usual calm, open, face clouded over. "I don't have much time, Carmen. They say we're going to get into the war in Europe any day now. If we do, I've gotta go, and Sheriff's Academy will have to wait. I need to do something soon."

Carmen cocked her pretty head, and wrinkled her forehead in thought. After a long pause, she spoke. "OK, I've got an idea. You know my brother, Steve? He goes to N. C. State. He's got an apartment in downtown Raleigh with some of his engineering buddies. If Becky can get out to go to the doctor, or something like that, maybe Steve can clear the apartment for y'all to meet."

With Carmen as a go-between, Buck and Becky made plans, but unfortunately, on April 6th, 1917, America declared war on Germany, and Buck soon found himself in boot camp at an army fort outside Raleigh. They were within twenty miles of each other but couldn't bridge the distance. Was everything stacked against them? Could they get so close and yet fail? A break finally came in the fall when wrestling came to the fort and Buck got pushed to the front to take on the Division champion.

"If I beat him, I want a two day pass," Buck said. And so the deal was made, and Buck got to meet Becky.

They met at Carmen's brother's apartment. Buck got there first and picked up the empty beer bottles and dirty clothes thrown on the floor, and then started pacing, waiting for her to come.

It had been so long since they had been together. When the knock finally came, Buck ran to the door. Becky stood there, her luminous eyes shining, wet with tears. They stood for a moment looking at each other, her in a green pleated skirt and canary yellow blouse with ruffles, and him in his plain, unadorned army drab uniform.

"B . . . Becky," he cried, and reached for her.

"Buck, Oh Buck."

He lifted her, but oh so gently, and carried her to the bed and placed her down on the edge facing him. He stood working clumsily at the buttons on his khaki shirt. She wriggled out of her skirt and reached for his belt, and his hands moved down to fight with hers as they struggled to undo it. Finally, they stood naked and panting, facing each other among the tangled jumble and snarl of their clothing. Without a word, their hands and mouths were on each other, and they were moving in the primitive mating ritual of primates from a million years ago. Her eyes were shut and lips parted when he lifted her and placed her on top of him. She felt him moving inside her, and in the last exhausting moment when she could continue no longer, she heard his deep sigh . . . but his last words clearly spoken: "Becky . . . Becky . . . Becky!"

In the late gloaming that precedes the pitch blackness of nightfall but well before her curfew, he watched her descend the stairs and cross the parking lot to the street. For a moment he was lost in reverie, detached, just watching a pretty girl with the classic motion of a model walk slowly away. Wouldn't it be wonderful if every guy had special girl like that, he thought? And suddenly he realized that he alone had won the ultimate prize. The swirl of strawberry hair and the indigo eyes that captured him from the beginning still shone in the darkness as she looked back and sadly waved goodbye.

On July 18th, 1918, the French launched a major attack on the Germans from the forest of Villers-Cotterets. Two American divisions of 54,000 men accompanied them. Buck Tindal was one of them. They came out from beneath the dark shadows of the trees, and charged across a meadow covered with wildflowers. It was there that Buck fell as he held his Springfield rifle high and charged through the exploding cannon rounds and machine gun fire. His blood stained the ground and flowed among the flowers.

When Buck awoke he was in a small hospital in Paris. He had been there for a week, lying amongst the bloody dying and the unmoving slain. There was a thick bandage over his left eye, and his face was swathed in gauze. His left leg was heavily bandaged up to his thigh, and there was a cast on part of it. A doctor and a nurse stood near him.

"On ne pensait pas quetu allait survivre," the Doctor said abruptly. "The severe concussion complicated things. You have lost your left eye, but you should be able to see with the other if we can remove the shrapnel from around it cleanly. The wound in your leg is bad. We can save it, I think, but you will need to recuperate for a long time. "Je suis mavre pour toi." With that he left.

The nurse was short and compact with auburn hair and expressive green eyes that fluttered in sync with her hands. She spoke in an almost breathless voice.

"My name is Marie," she said in halting English. "It is true you have lost an eye and are wounded in the leg, but you will heal and your life will go on . . .and, mmmm . . . tu retrouvera la joie de vivre."

As simple as these words sounded, Buck would never forget them and the true sound of them from the lips of Marie as she tried to arrange her thoughts in English. Could anything said in this bleakest moment of his life be more hopeful.

America had already sent 584,000 troops to counter the Germans' great offensive of March, 1918, and the hospitals were overflowing. Wounded soldiers came and went and some died, but Buck stayed on through the winter of 1918. The wounds were healing, but he was still blacking out from the concussion and had lost much of his memory of past events. After consultation with American doctors, he was moved to a specialty hospital where surgeons operated on his skull to relieve the pressure. In early 1919, Buck was transferred to a recovery center between the Luxembourg gardens and the River Seine. It had been converted from a military equipment storage warehouse. The windows were small and the lower ones were barred. In the summer and even into the fall, the heat would be oppressive, but now it was still chilly and he wore a sweater an anonymous patriot had knitted for him. It was there that he met Marie again.

In the early summer of 1919, when he had recovered to the point where he was once again mobile, Marie helped him walk through the Luxembourg gardens and along the quays on the Seine. They found a place below the Pont Neuf where the backwaters curled around a park with chestnut trees. There were always fishermen standing along the banks fishing with cane poles. Sometimes they cooked their catch on charcoal braziers, and Buck would bring several bottles of chilled chablis, and he and Marie would sit on the ground and eat with the fishermen, and Marie would translate. The fishermen were usually older and worked when they could and fished when they couldn't. It was especially fun on Sunday afternoon when the women and children came. The children ran and played, the women huddled and talked, and the men fished and smoked foul smelling cigarettes wrapped in brown paper; and people laughed and were happy.

1919 came and went. Buck was beginning to remember some of his past, and was teaching himself to write again. Mail from home finally began to reach him. His father had been ill. Walking too many miles for a Camel, his Mother said. Becky Stone. Whatever happened to Becky? Well, she had just vanished from the face of the earth several years ago. Nobody had any idea where she was. Big thing was, Becky's parents, the Stones, had been killed in an automobile accident; and wherever she was, she didn't have much left to come home to.

Buck was sitting in the recreation room of the stuffy old building where he lived with the other men who were recovering when mail call was announced. Marie was standing next to him when he was handed the letter. It had been posted two months earlier:

Dear Buck,

Thank God you're alive. I just found out. I kept waiting for you to write and when I didn't hear, I asked your daddy, and he said the family had been told you were missing in action and probably dead because the Army never could account for you. All I could do was cry, and I cried myself to sleep every night. I remember how much we loved each other, and I know that love never dies. That's why it hurts me in a way I can't describe to tell you I am now married and live on a farm with my husband and baby. Oh, Buck, I thought you were dead. Please forgive me Buck! Please!

All my love,
Becky

Marie took Buck in her arms and held his head tightly against her bosom. "Mon cher ami," she said. "My dear boy."

To Buck, for the moment, the music of those words spoken in French were all that mattered. He couldn't remember what Becky was talking about.

And then Marie told him her story, straightforward and without sentiment. "I also was in love. We were not married, but my mother loved him too, and she rented us an apartment above hers. But we paid no rent, you know. When he was killed in the trenches, I literally tore my hair out, and tried to commit suicide, but my faith saved me. A Nun held me, the way I am holding you now, and said, what I said to you before: 'Your life will go on, and you will be happy again.' And so it has."

A few days after the letter arrived, Marie took Buck to meet her mother. Madame Bouchard owned a house on a narrow cobblestone street near the Place de la Contrescarpe. The house had been converted into an awkward looking three-story apartment building with enclosed toilets at the head of each flight of stairs that were visible from the street.

Madame Bouchard was in the kitchen when Marie and Buck arrived. She was short and round and wore an apron on which she was constantly wiping her hands. She spoke no English and depended on Marie to translate, and was always smiling after Marie finished. Buck soon found out Madame Bouchard was a superb cook. Marie told him she was preparing *Poulet Poele A L'Estragon*, a casserole-roasted chicken dish with tarragon, and mushroom stuffing. Madame Bouchard opened a bottle of Bordeaux—Medoc wine that she had saved from before the war, and served them where they sat at the kitchen table. Buck kept telling Marie how good everything tasted, and Marie translated, and Madame Bouchard smiled and kept looking at Buck out of the corner of her eye.

She seemed to be looking the other way on the next visit when Marie took Buck into the rear bedroom. Marie slowly removed her clothes, letting him watch her undress and she lay upon the stuffed mattress, pulling Buck towards her. Her body was as Buck had thought: muscle hard with a wholesome peasant look about it, and when she wrapped her legs around him, he could feel the pressure constricting him like a jungle snake.

Later, they sat in a café in the corner and kissed and held hands and drank wine. There were Americans at a table nearby trying to order in French, and they laughed and Marie went over to help them.

When she rejoined him, she placed her hand on his arm. "Buck, I believe you will be discharged from the hospital soon. I want you to think about staying on in Paris, at least for the present. You don't have to do anything or go anyplace, For a while you can just experience life and let the rest go. Tu retrouveras la joie de vivre, tu verras. You will be happy again. You will see."

When Buck was discharged from the hospital, he came to live with Marie on the second floor of Madame Bouchard's building. Marie worked at the hospital while Buck strolled in the Strasbourg gardens and soaked up the culture along the Seine. He drank wine with expatriates in the cafes and sipped coffee and talked with the American writers at Sylvia Beach's bookstore. He took to wearing the tight, black, T-Shirts of the workers along the Seine and began to speak whatever he had learned of French. When he came home in the evening, he would eat Madame Bouchard's superb cooking and make love with Marie.

On an evening a year later Buck met her at the entrance to the apartment house. It had rained and now the air was clear and he could smell the ozone. There were horse drawn carts in the street bringing deliveries, and he could smell the dung, and all the odors of the evening clung together. Buck kissed her and raised her chin to look at him.

"This is hard for me to tell you Marie, but I have to go home," he said. "I have been happier with you than any words I know how to say, but I need to remember who I was before all this happened to me. I know I can't return and find it the way it was, but I need to go back and experience life there again if I'm ever going to have peace. And if there's anyway I can come back, I will."

Marie placed her head against his chest and cried. When she had finished she looked up at him.

"Finding you has meant so much to me Buck," she said. "I will miss hearing your voice, and coming home to find you waiting. Please, for both of us, do not feel sad. It is something we have learned. We will both be happy again"

When he left, he held her at arms length, squinting in the sunlight with his one good eye.

"As long as I live, Marie, I will never forget you and what we had together," he said.

"Ne t'inquiete pas tout ira bien, Go in peace," she whispered.

At the end of the cobblestone street he looked back to see her still standing there waving, her auburn hair glistening in the sun, a short, pretty French girl, who had given him herself and a future when he needed it.

Buck sat quietly next to Becky Porter, the knitting in his lap resting untouched. His apprehensions about the past and future had faded, and his mind was at rest when a moment of nostalgia crept in like a soft summer breeze. His thoughts turned to Marie Bouchard and he was remembering the fresh scent of her and the way she talked using her hands and eyes to give expression to what she was saying as well as her passion for making love and loving life.

Others moments of nostalgia followed and Buck was now

remembering a summer church camp for boys and girls he had attended. He was thirteen and he had never been as happy as he was with his new friends. He had a little girlfriend named Alice, and he swore to all he would return next year and even wrote down addresses and phone numbers. But as the days and months passed, Buck's interests turned elsewhere, and his experiences at summer camp faded in his memory. He never returned to see his friends and little girlfriend. Where were they all now, he wondered, and what did they look like, and what became of little Alice? He wondered the same thing about Marie. Caught up in a new life in the States after the war, and despite their letters to each other, Buck's passion for returning to France and Marie slipped away. He kept telling himself he would, but he never did. The memories stung, but he would be fine for now. Then a moment in time would come when the past would wash over him again, and he would marvel at the beauty of life remembered.

As Buck Tindal sat in reverie, a motion from across the room disturbed him. Across from him, Becky's sister, Lenore, had stopped rocking and plucking at the space around her, and now sat quietly mumbling to herself. Buck picked up his knitting with a look of utter frustration.

"Oh, come on, Buck," Becky said. She smiled as she moved next to him, and took his hands in hers. "The stitches are drawn more closely together in the heel, like this," she said as she guided his hands through the knitting of a gusset.

Buck turned to look at her with his one good eye and broke into a grin. "I don't know why you're doing this to me," he said.

Becky could contain herself no longer. She broke into stomach-bending, tear rending, laugh. When they had finished for the evening, they walked to the door, two middle-aged people saying goodbye. Her strawberry blond hair had dulled somewhat, and she had put on a little weight in the hips; but her indigo-blue eyes were clear and her face unblemished, and she walked with the same grace of a fashion model as she did thirty-five years ago. He had gained a small roll of weight around the middle that showed when he sat down, and his blond hair had begun to thin; but the shrapnel scars on his face and head had been fixed by plastic surgery so that all that was left of that disastrous infantry charge was the patch over his eye and the faintest hint of a limp.

Becky opened the door and he turned to face her, their merging silhouettes caught in the yellow light from the house. She reached up and drew Buck's head toward her and kissed him hard on the mouth, letting her lips and tip of her tongue rest on his longer than she intended.

Buck instinctively pulled her to him. They stood together, motionless statues caught in profile.

Becky was the first to push back. "Goodnight, Buck dear," she said. "Please take care of yourself, won't you?"

Buck dismissed her concern with a wave of his hand. "Goodnight B . . . Becky," he said, and turned and walked down the steps to his patrol car, the swagger in his gait that of a high school wrestling champion who had just been kissed by his favorite cheerleader.

PART FIVE

JUDGEMENT.

GOING DOWN

LUTHER RETURNS

When the mullet stopped jumping and the taste of salt was almost gone from his fingers, the large, muscle-bound man with the misshapen face knew he was close to the place where he would bring his Momma. He had not been there for more than eighteen years, and the river had seen some changes, but the presence of the narrow, hidden tributary was strong in his senses. But where was the entrance? Where was the black hole in the riverbank that would pull him into its depths and deposit him on the other side into the ankle-deep water covering the bar, the shallows that would lead to the navigable waterway and the old hunt camp? All the openings looked much the same. Some of the small creeks twisted and turned and found their way back to the river. Others, if you followed them, joined networks of maze-like canals where novice duck and marsh hen hunters had been lost for days, and a few, forever.

The key to finding the right spot was to spot the three old duck blinds that sat in the shallow water along a bend in the river. As long as anyone living could remember, they had stood there immune to hurricanes and time and had served as a refuge for boaters in bad weather. If one looked closely, it was clear that they formed a triangle, and it was at the nearest point to the river where an

157

observer could see what appeared to be an island of cattails, their brown hotdog-shaped spikes moving with the breeze or weighted down with resting blackbirds. It was there that the big man who sat in the stern pointed the small boat.

"O.K. Pender," Luther Quinn said to the dwarf-sized man with the startling blue eyes. "This is the spot."

Luther piloted the boat straight at the bank of cattails and ran aground in their midst. It was a dead end for anyone else, but Luther remembered. He knew exactly where he was.

"Here's where we get out and push," he said.

The gnome-like figure jumped out and got behind the boat.

Luther pulled up the fifty horsepower Johnson Seahorse outboard so it cleared the muddy bottom and began to push the sixteen foot flats boat through the cattail bed. On the other side, they entered a narrow canal that ended in a sea of marsh grass. It was as if the stalks were silent sentinels warning them to turn back.

"Luther, you sure we're gonna get there this way?" Pender asked.

Luther forced a smile

"Brother, have I ever let you down?" he said.

The route, blocked by a sandbar at low tide and hidden by marsh grass at high, had purposely been selected to discourage curious boaters from trying to get through the maze of canals to find the hunt camp. It was an alternate route seldom used, but that turned out to be lucky. When Luther was just a kid, long before he killed Cyrus, they would come this way, even though it was a longer route. Cyrus's official job was yard superintendent for the railroad, but during the hunting and fishing seasons he doubled as guide and camp manager for the railroad's executives and special guests and their women. The route that visitors were accustomed to was actually a detour from the main line to a switching station that shunted the engine and plush dining car to a deserted site where once rosin and turpentine were distilled from the abundant pine forest. It was less than a mile from there to the hunt camp, and that was managed with railroad push cars. Everything was great for all the bigwigs until the government built a huge ammunitions complex at the beginning of WWII and razed everything within forty miles including the switching station and tracks that led to the camp. That left only the river route and none of the ladies nor any of the forty-eight size belts would even think about going that way. The hunt camp experience soon died, and the camp itself lay vacant.

Luther's smile faded. He had spent almost two decades in that goddamn prison waiting, and locating the hunting camp was the first step. He had to be alert. He turned his attention back to the marsh grass. It was beginning to thin out and he could see a waterway up ahead, but no building. Had he somehow missed the one canal among hundreds? Suddenly cranes and marsh hens began to scatter and fly in front of the boat. After being unaccustomed for so many years to a boat this close to their feeding and nesting grounds, there they were, leading the way as if they had been suddenly appointed as escorts to royal visitors.

Then he saw it facing the canal like a proud hostess welcoming her guests.

"There it is Pender," Luther shouted. "There it is!"

The building was exactly as he remembered it. It had been built from planks hewn from oak, hickory and pine on the property. The railroad chiefs couldn't take a chance on outsiders seeing large amounts of building materials being dropped off at the junction. Newspaper reporters would be all over the place, so handpicked railroad construction workers did it themselves.

A Time Before the End

Luther moved through the building recalling the way it was laid out. Dust and mildew covered the place, and the droppings of animals that had broken in covered the floor. It would take time to clean up, but Luther was enthusiastically up to the task. He was home!

He almost couldn't believe he had pulled it off—the escape from a prison you weren't supposed to escape from. After running like hell, coming up on the rear of a huge sea of junkyard vehicles on the outskirts of Raleigh where they found an old, ramshackle Chevy pickup, that after a bit of effort was running again. How did they ever get it started, anyway? Evading the Highway Patrol, the local police, the sheriff's deputies, and all the roadblocks and then hiding the truck in the back of a wooded lot that backed up to the river. Who'd ever think of it? Finally, him and Pender walking like peacocks along the bank until they spotted a boat with a key in the ignition. It was all too good to be true, but then it was true, and Luther knew his time had come. All the years in prison ended. All the time away from his Momma ended. All the time without revenge ended. Providence had given Luther this opportunity, and he was going to make the most of it.

PENDER RENEGES

The crack of gunshots echoed in the early morning stillness. Pender bolted upright and looked around. For a moment he couldn't remember where he was, and the gunfire frightened him. He ran to a secluded corner of the room and crouched like an animal startled by a sudden noise. The shadow of a black bear's head fell on him. He started to sweat. His breathing came in pants. Pender was terrified. Then he remembered. He had gone to sleep on a couch in the hunt camp's trophy lounge. He crept to the screen door on all fours in his monkey walk and peered out. He sat crouched until Luther appeared on the porch carrying a twenty-two-caliber rifle and three dead squirrels.

"I told you I wasn't going to let you starve, baby," Luther said playfully.

Luther started a fire with a piece of flint rock using an old jack handle as a striker and the powder from one of the .22 cartridges he had found with the gun. He quartered the squirrels and coated them with flour he had ground from the heads of some cattails he had picked and then cooked on the wood stove. He had also dug up some wild legumes and threw them into the mix as well. He had learned the survival skills as a young boy from his daddy Cyrus.

When they had finished eating, Luther pushed back from the bare table and looked at Pender.

"You was born near here, wasn't you?" he said.

"You know I was," Pender said. "I told you before. You just forgot. We gotta be in Brunswick County now. Pender County is next to Brunswick. Named after some Confederate officer. A Baptist preacher found me naked, except for my diapers, sittin' beside the road on the Pender County Line. That's how I got my name. Old preacher Brown—Seth was his name—picked me up and took me home. Seems he and his wife never had kids, and that's where I lived until I ran away. He was the calmest and most patient guy I ever met until he got up to preach, and then he was somethin' else. He would prance around the stage, screaming about the evils of booze, smoking, and women he called hussies. I never seen anythin' like it. His face would get all red, and he kept flingin' his arms like he was havin' a fit or somethin'. I thought he would bust a gasket, which he finally did. And the funny thing was, all the pallbearers stood outside smokin' until it was time to carry the casket in. Old Mrs. Brown, she just fell apart. Couldn't figure out what to do without him. They musta been married young cause she wasn't all that old, but the way she fixed her hair and the long dresses she wore, you would think she was a hundred. You can't believe how dull it was livin' there with her covered up from head to toe, and him calling her 'Mother'. I had the room next to them, and if they ever had sex, I didn't hear it. I tried to hang in but it got so depressin' with the way she kept mumbling' and twistin' a handkerchief into knots and wearin' that black veil everywhere that I had to move on. And you know what I found out? The freaks I worked with at the circus were a hell lot happier than she was, and they knew how to have fun and didn't take themselves all that seriously. They never went to church neither.

"Anyway, you know all the rest. If it hadn't been for that second-story job I tried to pull off in Winston-Salem, I'd be back with a circus somewhere. Even after the escape, if you hadn't killed the guard, I'd still be out in a few years. But you went and did it, and now if they catch me, I'll be in for life. Maybe even get the chair. So my life's fucked up for good. Best thing I can do now is join up with one of those gypsy troupes. I'd fit right in with their routines. They get knocked for stealing' and stuff like that, but they're loyal as hell to their own kind and they'd keep me safe. So yeah, I'm close to where I was born, but I left that place a long time ago."

Luther gave Pender a sly, crooked smile. "I don't know how I'm ever going to do without you, brother," he said.

That morning after they ate, they cleaned the lodge. With the dirty, backbreaking job finished, they sat on the porch and rocked. It seemed that for the first time in a long while Luther was at peace. Pender decided it was his best chance to try to make a break from the mess he was in.

"I'm glad you're goin' to see your Momma," he said. It's been a long time, too long for a man not to see his Momma. Course, I never knew who mine was. Figured she was in a traveling circus somewhere and knew she couldn't keep me. Anyway, that's the way I like to look at it. Tell you what, Luther. Maybe when you leave to go see your Momma, you can drop me off on Highway 17 south of town, and I'll make my way down to Myrtle Beach. I hear they got a lot of gypsy run places down there, and maybe they can hook me up with a circus where they don't ask too many questions. Maybe I can even find my own momma, if she's still alive. How about it, Luther? You got to cross 17 to get out of here."

Luther reached over and dragged Pender from the chair and forced him to his knees, a giant hand squeezing his small throat.

"Listen runt. I'm gonna do what I planned ever since I hit the damn prison. I'm gonna get Momma and take her someplace where they can't find us, 'cept she's too sick now so I'm bringing her here and I need you to help me. You're not going anywhere Pender!"

Luther looked straight ahead, eyes unfocused, oblivious to the grunts Pender was making and the hairy ape-like hands he was using to free himself. Strong hands were Pender's stock in trade because you couldn't climb and swing without them. He broke the grip on his throat, but he had to do something to break Luther's trance-like state. Words were his only choice.

163

"So whatcha goin' to do when the cops close in? You'll be trapped."

Luther squinted and looked at Pender. He thought hard about what he was going to say.

"Funny you should ask that Pender, and I can't tell you much. It ain't healthy, if you know what I mean. First thing I'm going to do when I get her here is make her comfortable and tell her how much it means for us to be together again. Wish we could go off some place far away but we can't. The main thing is we've had this time together and that's something nobody can take away from us.

"But to answer your question, Pender, I'll stay until I see the cranes, marsh hens, and ducks beginning to stir down toward the river or hear the 'copters closing in. Then I'll tell Momma I've got to leave so I won't be caught, but somebody will be coming soon to take her home. I got a way planned out the back way toward the old rosin and turpentine place, and nobody will be able to trace me after I get there."

Luther knew he was talking too much, but he was in a euphoric mood. He couldn't restrain himself.

"Well, I guess I *can* tell you this much, Pender. There's a couple of places in South America I'm looking at. One is in Argentina where a lot of Nazis holed up near the end of the War; and they can sure use somebody like me. Then there's this river in Brazil called the Amazon, where a guy can get lost even if he doesn't want to. They got mostly small people down there, and a big guy like me could take over and live like a king. I'll probably be going to one of those places, but I got to travel by myself so I don't draw too much attention, if you know what I mean."

Pender knew what he meant.

CROSSROADS

Ben Porter opened his eyes and lay still. He was waiting, waiting to cringe if the dream monster chose to visit him so close to first light. Waiting for the beast called death to appear at the corner of his memory. Waiting to feel the sweat-drenched sheets against his body, or catch the odor of urine. But no, this morning he was clear of the post-traumatic shock he had been experiencing. There was, however, something else, a *reality*, not a past event but equally as horrifying that began to crowd out all of his other thoughts. Luther was on the loose, prowling the land, searching for him and Olive.

He could hear Sarah moving around in the small kitchen in the manager's living quarters of the motel. Funny for her to be up so early, but the events of the last few days had unnerved her. The sex they had last night had been filled with the frenetic motions of bonding that come in times of danger, but even then Sarah had to work to make it satisfactory. He didn't understand it. A good look-ing girl like her wanting to hook up with a screwed up veteran who couldn't get it up half the time. It didn't make any sense, but then, not much else that was happening did either. Ben shook his head, slipped out of bed and pulled on a pair of jeans and a loose, but colorful Hawaiian shirt and walked into the kitchen.

Sarah had brewed coffee and was getting out a frying Pan. She smiled and kissed Ben on the cheek.

"I guess you're still going," she said

"I wasn't, but with Buck putting a deputy on the front desk, I think we'll be all right. Luther's probably holed up waiting for all the activity to die down. Anyway, I need to go. They've ok'd it for me to see this woman doctor at Duke that deals with dreams. They can't do it at the VA so I'm going to have to go to Durham."

Rachel, with her cap of curly black hair and hazel eyes, still in her pajamas, sauntered in and wrapped her arms around him.

"What're you girls going to do while I'm gone?" Ben asked.

"We're not telling," Sarah said, suppressing a smile.

Rachel giggled. "We always do secret things while you're gone."

A mock expression of parental anger clouded Ben's face. "Just wait till I find out," he said. "No more jellybeans for you."

The three of them broke out laughing, and Ben pulled Sarah and Rachel into his arms.

"I think we're going into town and catch a movie," Sarah confessed. "That should be safe enough. I'll have something nice for dinner waiting for you."

"I always eat seconds while you're gone," Rachel said, pulling away before Ben could fake a move to retaliate.

Ben released Sarah with a kiss and she moved to the refrigerator, and Rachel moved to help her.

"We'll fix you some breakfast and pack a sandwich for lunch," Sarah said

Ben had what he wanted, a woman to love and a child to nourish.

A sheriff's deputy wearing a neat white shirt and tie had taken over the registration counter. He nodded to Ben and Sarah as they made their way through the small lobby to the exit.

"I got it covered, Mr. Porter," the deputy said as they passed.

Sarah gave Ben a kiss and he walked through the door towards his car, swinging the brown bag that held his lunch. He was humming as he drove out of the parking area towards the crossroads.

Luther was driving carefully so as to not draw attention to himself. He had come too far to slip up now. He had sent Pender into the A&P Food Store to steal some old lady's purse from a cart while she was looking around, so they had some money for food and gas; but that wasn't what was on Luther's mind. In ten minutes they would be at his Aunt Becky's house. That's where his Momma was.

Luther remembered the night he saw Lenore through the crack in the door.

"My Momma's beautiful. You'll see Pender," he said. When they came to a large crossroads, Luther pointed. "Hanover is straight ahead. That road there, that's 17. Takes you straight down to Myrtle Beach. That's where you wanted to go," he said, and jabbed Pender in the ribs. "That road over there, that's 421 that takes you to Carolina Beach and down where Ben has that motel. After I get my momma safe, I'm coming back for that boy."

"You gonna take that kind of chance," Pender said. "Don't seem to me that it'd be worth it."

Luther pounded the dashboard with his fist.

"You don't know the whole story, Pender," he said. "Ben and the nigger didn't have to let themselves get drawn into it. Then Ben came with the sheriff when he came to arrest me, and started talking to me about giving myself up like he was a deputy or something, and Momma having to look at it and then her having that breakdown. Damn right I'm going to get back at him and her too if I get the chance. You do something against me you're going to pay for it. That's the way I've always been, Pender."

When they reached the neighborhood, Luther parked the truck around the corner from Becky's house, and he and Pender walked where they could see it. A deputy sheriff's car sat in front.

"Damn it, they're guarding the house," Luther said.

"But I don't see anybody inside," Pender said.

"O.K., the guy must be inside the house. I been inside that house a hundred times. Come on. We'll go in the back way."

Luther led Pender down a back alley past two adjoining houses and came to the back yard of Becky's home. They edged up to the rear and Luther climbed five concrete steps to a screened porch. He flexed his fingers to relax them. He tried the door. It was locked. He slit the screen with his knife and unlocked the door. He tried the door to the house. Damn it, it was locked too. Pender had the answer. How many locks had he jimmied on his way to prison?

Luther slipped inside and stood quietly listening to the sounds of the house. There were noises coming from the parlor.

"Here's what we're gonna do," he told Pender.

They crept down the hall. Luther moved slowly, heel to toe in order to distribute his weight evenly. Pender followed with his ape-like moves, as silent as a spider crossing a web.

As they approached the parlor, Luther heard the voice of his aunt Becky. She was somewhere in the interior of the room saying something about an Indian summer and how she was looking forward to some really cool weather. Then the deputy spoke. He was standing next to the door of the parlor, not five feet from Luther. Luther drew a filet knife from a leather sheath on his belt. He took three steps and wrapped his huge hand over the deputy's mouth and pulled his head back. It was over in three ticks from the Grandfather clock that stood nearby. The deputy lay dying with a slash across his jugular. Pender had his hand over Becky's mouth and his long arm wrapped around her so she could not move.

"OK, Aunt Becky, where's my Momma," Luther said, and then he saw someone sitting in the far corner.

Who was that sitting there? That dried up old hag couldn't be his Momma! Luther edged closer to look at her. He craned his long neck to get a better angle. Her once unfurled auburn hair, exploding with highlights as it lay moving on the sea-swell of her bosom, hung in gray strings and tangles over hunched shoulders and sagging breasts. Her fingers, so elegantly shaped and poised as a young woman, lay in her lap twisted by inflammation into clawing witches' talons. Her skin, so smooth and firm when she held him as a child, was now wrinkled and reddened from eczema and scratching; her temples scarred from the effects of electric shock therapy. Her hazel eyes, once so expressive, so alive, now were dead.

But it was his Momma, all right. "Momma, Momma, look what they done to you." Luther cried. "Oh Momma, Momma."

Lenore gave Luther a crooked smile and pulled back her lips to show a row of yellow teeth.

Becky wrenched one hand loose and pulled Pender's hand from her mouth.

"Your mother is dying, you fool," She shouted at Luther. "It's all the electric shock and medicine, and now look what you've done."

Luther dropped down in front of Lenore. He caught the odor as he settled on his knees. He had smelled it before. The stench of death was in the air. He lowered his head onto her lap and placed her hand on his hair and felt her ever-moving fingers in it. He rested his head on her breasts one last time. He started to cry. A squeal tore from his throat like that of a lamb being slaughtered.

"Goodbye, Momma," Luther wailed.

A SONG FOR LENORE

The day that Lenore Quinn died, the bird of dawn that sang in the mulberry tree outside her window began to sing all through the night, its forlorn dirge saturating the dark corners of the house. It was Lenore's custom to sit in her special chair in the small parlor rocking to and fro to an unsteady cadence, stopping only long enough to pick at her hair or dress, or shuffle down the hall to the toilet accompanied by her sister Becky. Sometimes when the medication wore off, she would become agitated and pace the floor making wild gestures until Becky came to comfort her and return her to the worn cushion of the chair.

But the afternoon that Lenore died something was different. A calm had come over her. She settled herself in her chair; and when the bird perched on the branch outside the window and began its final song, Lenore Quinn fell asleep to its music and had her last dream.

Lenore stood before the altar in her royal gown, her diadem of gold and inlaid jewels held by both hands at her waist. The interior of the sanctuary held no pews or books of prayer or ornaments of any kind. It was empty except for what was built covering an octagonal shaped mosaic on the floor. The mosaic's design was based on the pattern built into the floor of Chartres Cathedral in France during the 13th century. It was a labyrinth used for contemplative prayer and had only one path leading to the center—closest to the Godhead—and out along the same route. Pilgrims came from far and wide to meditate along its intricate mosaic path.

But recently a structure had been built to cover the mosaic and its path had been changed to form a maze with routes so convoluted that no one who had entered ever emerged. Even the architect and builder had been unfortunately trapped by his own creation.

The maze had been built to contain a monstrous creature who had recently risen from the mucky slime of the swamp—one so stunningly beautiful that women swooned at its sight and men turned away, but so foul in its concupiscent habits that it could never live outside the confines of the maze. Since its emergence from the swamp, the creature's appetite had become ravenous, and now it was only satisfied when fed the fairest maidens from far and wide who were brought to the doors of solid gold and locked inside. But the creature had recently stopped feeding and now roared day and night so loud that its terrifying sounds could be heard throughout the kingdom. Lenore's subjects were increasingly afraid, and she had to do something about it.

One night a vision of the creature came to her in her sleep. It was so beautiful she had to turn her head away for fear of madness but so disgusting in its carnal desire that she shuddered. It bent and whispered to her, and Lenore knew what the ultimate sacrifice would have to be in order to save her subjects. With tears streaming down her face, she placed her crown on the altar and walked to the golden doors of the maze and knocked. A sound of insatiable pleasure came from within.

≋

The bird that sang at the window was gone. Only Luther's demanding cry for his Momma was left in its place.

Luther walked up and down in front of Becky who was now standing free of restraint in front of him. She looked at him without fear, her indigo blue eyes unblinking and hard.

"Just look at my Momma over there," Luther shouted, thrusting his distorted face nose to nose with hers. Blood vessels in his temples pulsated as he tried to control his rage. "Look what you all done to her."

"We didn't do anything to Lenore but take care of her," Becky said. "You know that Luther. She was always delicate, and couldn't cope with what happened."

Luther's face turned red. He grabbed Becky by the throat.

"Please don't hurt her," Pender blurted out. "She ain't done nothing."

"Shut up, runt. They all knew what they did to my Momma when they testified against me."

Luther slowly loosened his grip on Becky's throat. He managed a crooked grin.

"Tell you what, Aunt Becky. If I didn't have something else in mind for you, I'd kill you right now. But I'm going someplace, and you're going with me."

THE MESSAGE

The sun sat heavy on the horizon when Ben left Duke University Medical Center. He didn't like to travel after dark. As if they were a portent, the long shadows of the evening hours brought to Ben a foreboding sense of impending peril. He knew the day would soon wind down and the bed confront him, and then what dreams might come when he fell asleep. That's what he would be working on with the new psychiatrist—the demons that crawled into his head once he went to sleep. They called her a Jungian analyst, someone who specialized in dream work. That's what he needed, for sure.

He pushed the '49 Ford pickup as fast as he dared to beat the growing darkness, but the night had closed in on him when he finally passed through the crossroads and took the blacktop toward Carolina Beach. Once he crossed over the inlet and hit the Beach's city limit, he turned south along the narrow strip of highway towards the motel. There it was, dead ahead, its happy welcoming 'SEA OATS' sign glowing in the dark. Ben was smiling as he made the final turn into the parking lot. But what were three sheriff's cruisers doing parked haphazardly in front of the motel entrance with their lights flashing? What was going on here?

Ben jumped from the truck and headed towards the lobby. He had not taken five steps when he ran into a man so black he was almost invisible in the darkness—a huge figure, towering far above Ben, his outstretched arm restraining him.

"You hold up, Mister Ben," Black James said.

Ben grabbed James's massive arm, as deeply colored as an eggplant's skin. "James, what's wrong!" he cried out.

"Mister Ben, your cousin Luther done been here, killed the guard and take Miss Rachel away. He hurt Miss Sarah and your Momma."

Ben's eyes opened wide. Panic found its way into them and spread across his face.

"Oh, God. How bad is it?"

"Your Momma, she mainly shook up. Got some bruises where they tie her up. Miss Sarah, Luther done take her in the bedroom, you know, he hurt her pretty bad. She at the hospital. All the rest, they at Miss Carly's. They want you to come soon as I find you."

Ben and Black James stepped into the dimly lighted Voodoo parlor of Miss Carly Delome's house. Before them stood Ben's mother Becky, Olive Mills, Buck Tindal, and Miss Carly. Becky had the blank stare of a witness in shock. Her pale face was stripped of emotion. She had her arms crossed to cover the bruises. Buck had his arms around her, but his face showed no emotion either, only the hard fixed look of one ready to fight. Olive's eyes were puffy from crying, and she held a handkerchief against her mouth. Miss Carly, who had battled evil spirits for a long time, had a look of anger so intense that it seemed to consume all other feelings in the room.

Ben went to Becky and took her hands in his.

"Oh Momma," he said.

Becky's slow staccato voice bounced off the walls. "We . . .

are . . . going . . . to get . . . her . . . back." she said.

"Ben, we've got no time to waste," Buck said. "I know you want to see Sarah, but she's in good hands, and we've got to get on top of this thing right now. Luther left a message with your mother."

Becky turned to Ben. "Ben, Luther said the only reason he let me live was to bring a message to you. He's gone mad, of course. Took my car and strapped poor dead Lenore in beside him. Kept talking to her like she was still alive. Rachel and I had to sit in back with that Pender creature. Anyway, here's the message. He says only you and Olive can rescue Rachel. If he catches anyone else trying, he will kill her right then. No FBI, no police, nobody except the two of you. He's taken her someplace in the woods where you can get to by water. Buck thinks it's the old hunt camp the railroad people built 'round the turn of the century."

"You used to be able to get to the place easy," Buck said, "but when they built the munitions depot during the war, they tore out most of the railroad track and trestles. You can't get there that way anymore. James here says there's supposed to be a way through the canals that cut through the marsh, but nobody seems to know where it is except Luther, and he ain't saying. He says he'll let you know how to find him once you and Olive hit the river, but the only way to get to Rachel is through him. Like Becky says, he's crazy as a loon, and that's what makes him so unpredictable. And Ben, he says you and Olive got only two days to get there. You know what that means? You guys got to get your stuff together right now and leave at daybreak."

"Sheriff, why don't you bring in the FBI," Ben said.

"That's what I started to do right off, but when I began to think about it, I could see it wouldn't work with Luther. Counting my two deputies, he's already killed three law officers. Know what they do to people who kill just one law officer? Luther's not going to let himself be taken alive. If he gets wind of anybody but you and Olive looking for him, he's going to kill Rachel and run. That's what I think."

"But Buck, the FBI's trained to handle this kind of thing," Ben said.

"Well Ben. Let's look at it. FBI's got four choices: One, they can try to bargain with Luther. Even if they could somehow get close enough without him killing Rachel, they don't have anything to bargain with. I mean, with the guys I know around here, what's the chance he's going to get out of the woods alive. If he does, think any jury's going to let him off with a life sentence.

"Two, FBI or Airborne can try to parachute guys in and catch him by surprise. Guess what Luther's going to do if he hears planes? Suppose somehow they get away with it. Where they going to land? In the swamp or marsh with gators big enough to swallow a man alive, or water moccasins with fangs so deadly they'd kill a man before he could blink twice.

"Three, FBI or special ops can send guys in on foot. Place is surrounded on three sides by marsh and swamp, and thick woods covers the rest for miles and miles; and the access to the woods is through a government installation. Christ, do you know what kind of red tape you'd have to go through before you could start out. Rachel would be long dead by then, and, hell, Luther would be on his way to *wherever*.

"And, finally, four, forget trying to starve him out and finding Rachel alive. Luther knows how to live off the land. Don't forget, he lived with his daddy in those woods before he killed him. He can track a deer or bear or kill a gator as good as Davy Crockett or Daniel Boone.

"Think about it Ben. He's lost the only thing his cold heart ever cared about, and that's his Momma. He doesn't have anything else to live for. He's not going back to jail. He's obviously not afraid of dying, and he doesn't have a conscience. He's holding all the cards. FBI can't reach him in time. All he wants is you and Olive, and mainly you."

Ben dropped his arms in defeat. Trying to find another way out was a lost cause, but he still wasn't going to face it.

"Buck, you know all he wants to do is kill Olive and me. We'll be walking into a trap. There's got to be a better way."

"Hold on." Olive walked to the center of the room and stood next to Buck and Becky. She turned to Ben.

"She just happens to be my daughter too. I'm going after Rachel whether you do or not, Ben."

Ben felt Olive's dark eyes boring into him, saw the set of her jaw, the lift of her chin. He knew how Olive could act when she had her mind set on something.

"Olive, all I'm saying is that the FBI might have resources we don't know about, and they're better prepared to deal with things like this. That's all I'm saying."

"Am I hearing you right, white boy!" Olive said, placing her hands on her hips and giving Ben a withering look. "You saying to me, her mother, who you don't seem to want to have anything to do with, you don't want to go rescue our daughter. That you want to leave it up to the FBI or the PO'lice who are more interested in capturing Luther than rescuing our daughter. Is that what you're telling me, white boy!"

Ben's eyes dropped. For a moment he just stared at his feet. "I love my daughter and you all know it, but the after effects from the war have almost ruined me. I can't stand any more killing. That's all."

They all were standing silently looking at Ben when Miss Carly took over.

"Ben," she said softly. "I think you should go see Sarah, and when you're finished come back and talk with me."

Ben walked into the hospital room and found Sarah sitting in a chair. She wore a gown and was sitting with her hands in her lap looking at the wall.

Ben knelt in front of her and took her hands in his. "I love you," he said.

Sarah moved her eyes toward him. They were as hollow as if they had been branded on each side of her nose.

"I feel so dirty," she said. "I don't think I will ever feel clean again."

179

"I should have been there with you," he said. "I should have left Duke earlier."

"Its better this way," she said. "He's so big and violent, and he was looking for you. He just took it out on me and he did let me live."

"Let's get you out of here. I want to take you home," Ben said.

"It's already planned. I'm going home with Becky for now. Besides, I heard what Luther told Becky, the message to you and Olive. You've got to save Rachel."

"That's the thing, Sarah. I'm not the one to save her. I would just mess it up and get us all killed. I told them. Bring in the FBI."

"Ben! He's going to kill her if you don't go yourself."

Ben's face twisted in pain. He turned his eyes to the floor. "You know what seeing my crew slaughtered did to me, and what I went through in the Stalag, and the effect that all of that has had on you and me and even Rachel. I can't take violence anymore. It would destroy me."

Sarah looked at Ben and a deep sadness settled within her. "Ben, look at me. Our intimacy was brutally violated by Luther, and just like what happened to you in the war, I don't know when I'll ever feel good about things again. The thought that hurts me most is Rachel being in the hands of that monster and him doing the things to her that he did to me. As much as I have loved you Ben, I can tell you it will destroy what we have if you don't go. And Ben, you know you won't be able to live with yourself if anything happens to her that you could prevent. You will be dead, one way or the other."

Ben stood silently before Sarah.

Becky had entered the room and stood listening to the conversation. When she spoke, it was as if Ben were a stranger.

"Sarah, we best be going," she said, and she stepped around Ben to help Sarah from the chair. Neither Sarah nor Becky spoke to Ben, and they left him standing there alone.

THE LAST DANCE

When the others had left, Carly moved from place to place around the room touching each piece of furniture, moving this one a few inches, another a few feet, positioning all of them exactly as they had been before the meeting. After all, for over twenty years it was in this room that she had met with her sacred Loa, the spirits she believed inhabited all of nature and were responsible for the care of the universe. It was here in dreams or while in a trance that the Loa spoke to her and directed her activities. The Loa liked order. She had to have the room organized the way the Loa liked it. All was quiet except for the stirring of Olive in the kitchen and the squawk of the back door spring as Black James returned from his trip to Becky Porter's. Carly waited. When she was finally satisfied that a stillness had come to the house, she lowered herself into her rocker and slowly began the motion that would open the floodgate to her memories and reflections

How long had it been since the last dance, the last time she had circled the *poto mitan* with the sounds of the bongo drums and the haunting voices of the sweet *Loa* in her ears? Ten years? More? Had it really been that long? She tried to remember. Luther had been convicted and sent to prison. Then the war had come and Ben had gone to flight school before being sent to England to fly the big bomber they called the flying fortress.

A Time Before the End

The war had turned everything upside down for Carly. Her world before the war could not be re-created in the post war period. The small circus that had made its camp nearby was gone. Folks in Dry Pond who had suffered through the Great Depression had gone to work in the munitions depot or shipyard or some other war-related enterprise. Even the gypsies had gone to work in the war effort, and James had taken a night job on the production line of a weapons factory. Voodoo, which had been the faith of the poor and dispossessed was now relegated to show-time staged events for the curious in places like New Orleans and the famous festival in Sucre, Haiti. Her skills as a renowned spiritual medium that once brought large crowds to the Voodoo ceremonies at Hanover were now confined to fortunetelling and the selling of trinkets to the superstitious. It was her daughter, Olive, who had taken over the job as breadwinner in the family. All Carly had left were her memories, and she spent more and more time in the special chair where she met with the Loa. The inactivity had caused her to put on weight, and now there was a problem with an irregular heartbeat.

Yes, the Voodoo ceremonies were gone and her faith had been challenged by atheists and Christian dogmatists, but her belief in the Loa had somehow survived. Now in the midst of the worst crisis of her life she would call on them again. She would perform her last dance and call on the Loa to lend their supernatural aid to Ben and Olive and return Rachel to safety.

She went to the wall with all its ornaments. Not one had been replaced in all the years she had lived in the house. She reached high on the wall and removed the scabbard holding the long knife with the golden hilt. It had been a gift from a wealthy patron when she, as a young woman in Haiti, had risen to the status of a Voodoo priestess. It had never been used and only removed from its scabbard to burnish its twelve-inch hand-tooled blade and polish the hilt of gold and tighten the cap that covered a secret receptacle. Finally, Carly had a purpose for it. The Loa had known all along that one day she would need the knife. She took it down from the wall. Slowly, she removed the knife from the scabbard. Its polished steel flashed as she hefted it to check its balance. The hollow gold handle felt light in her palm but, then, that would soon be remedied. As she placed her palm against the cutting edge, she could feel the blade cut into her flesh and draw blood. Yes, it was a fine weapon to offer to the Loa for their blessing.

She called Olive into the room

"I am going to the old ceremonial grounds," she said. "Ben should be leaving the hospital by now. When he comes, bring him there."

"With your health and everything else going on, why're you going to do that, Momma?" Olive asked.

"I'm going, and that's the end of it," Carly said. "You can drive me and James as far as the path into the woods and then come back and wait for Ben."

Miss Carly stepped across the room to a cupboard and removed an ancient carpetbag. In it she placed a half bottle of rum and a bag of cornmeal. She pulled a shawl over her shoulders and picked up a battery-powered lantern, and stepped out into the night. Dark clouds driven by an angry wind scudded across the dome of the sky. Olive backed her newly purchased Plymouth down the gravel driveway and slowly pulled away with James and Miss Carly, who detested driving anywhere when she could walk. The path to the ceremonial grounds had changed since the last time she had walked it. Olive drove down an asphalt road that once had been dirt, and came to the entrance of a small housing development. Once, it had been a field where the circus set up its tents. Olive drove down its streets until they ended on a two-lane asphalt road that wound its way up a long incline to the top of the hill. The road had not been there when Carly, thirty pounds lighter, had hiked easily through the brush on a narrow path to the plateau where the spirit filled ceremonies began.

Olive shifted into second gear and began her climb. Halfway to the top she pulled over onto the right side shoulder of the road. Miss Carly got out with James helping her and moved laboriously along the shoulder until she came to a mark beside the road. She veered right and traversed a narrow path until she finally came to the clearing that had once been the ceremonial grounds. It lay enveloped in a thin ground fog. The wind blown clouds opened and closed around the moon causing a flickering light like that coming from a distant star. Beneath the fog, the underbrush had taken over—except for the dance route where over the years thousands of feet had obliterated every growing thing and left only the packed earth as a silent testament. Carly could almost hear the pounding feet and the cries of the dancers. She walked to the center of the circle where the *poto mitan* once stood and placed the lantern next to it. She cleared a place in the brush and spread cornmeal on the ground and poured rum on it. She did not have an animal to sacrifice, but she believed she had something in place of an animal that would please the Loa.

Who were the special Loa she would invite to the ceremony— the spirits who would bless the knife with power. First, she would invite *Ougon*, the warrior spirit, strong and dominant, and violent when he had to be. Next would be *Legba*, the gatekeeper to the world of the invisibles. Without him, Carly could not reach out to the other spirits. She would invite his counterpart, *Kalfu*, a Petro spirit who was the gatekeeper to the world of the angry, mean, dangerous Loa, the Loa of black magic used for death curses and the making of zombies. She did not like to be in the company of Petro spirits, but this time she needed the dark forces to help defeat Luther and save Rachel. She invited *Erzula*, who was the special spirit with whom she slept, and many others whom she felt would lend aid to her cause. She inscribed all their signs in the rum-soaked cornmeal, then took the knife with the golden hilt and drew its razor sharp edge across her arm. She let her blood run onto the cornmeal and mixed it in with the scribbled signs. This would be her sacrifice. Carly was ready for her last dance.

When Ben arrived at Miss Carly's home, he was surprised to see Olive on the porch, standing, waiting. She ran to him and took him by the arm.

"Momma is up at the ceremonial grounds," she exclaimed. "She has all her Voodoo paraphernalia with her. She says she's going to dance and ask the spirits to help us get Rachel back. She wants you there. Ben, she's not well enough for that kind of physical activity. We've got to go now."

Ben, Olive, and Black James stood at the edge of the clearing staring in amazement at Miss Carly. She held the large knife above her head and slashed at the night as her heavy body lurched forward in contorted dance steps around the *poto mitan*. She rounded the circle and came toward them. Blood poured from slashes on her arms where she had turned the knife on herself. Spit bubbled at the corners of her mouth. They could see she was in a trance.

"God, look at her," Olive said, and stepped onto the path.

Ben caught her arm and pulled her to him.

"Don't get in the way of the knife," he said.

As if a heavy weight had suddenly been placed on her back, Carly bent over at the waist and stumbled forward. A loud cry ripped from her twisted lips. On she plunged, swinging the knife in front of her. Suddenly, her body went limp. She fell to the ground. Her eyes rolled back until only the white showed. Leaves and dirt filled her mouth. She tried to rise but could not straighten her body. Ben, Olive, and James rushed to her. Olive was crying and James knelt and gently placed Carly's head on her lap. Ben reached down and picked up the blood-stained knife where it had fallen.

The last dance had ended.

Carly opened her eyes and looked into the terrified faces above her. Her ragged breathing filled the silence of the night. She felt a dull pain in her chest. Her arms burned from the cuts. The muscles in her arms and legs ached. But her mind was fixed on only one thing—the ultimate question. Had the Loa bestowed their power on the knife? Perhaps her special Loa, *Erzuli*, the earth mother, the spirit of love and beauty, would come to her in her pain and whisper the answer in her ear. They had only two days to save Rachel.

"Ben, I have asked my spirits to put their power into the knife," Carly said. "But only if you carry it in your search for Rachel will the power be yours. It will not work for anyone else." She pulled Ben's head toward her and whispered into his ear. He quickly pulled away, a startled expression on his face. "Lift up the knife, Ben!" Miss Carly said.

Olive looked at Ben. Ben stared at the knife.

"Lift up the knife and claim the power to save Rachel," Carly demanded.

A Time Before the End

Ben's hand holding the knife began to shake. Too much pain had been caused by his refusal to go, and now he was faced with the decision again. Could they possibly find Rachel in time? Slowly Ben raised the knife in his right hand and crossed it until it was over his heart.

THE SECRET

Ben stood on the floating dock in his Air Force flight jacket looking at the eighteen-foot center console fishing boat. The first splash of reddish color had touched the horizon. "Red sky at morning, sailors take warning," he thought. It could be a rough day on the water. Bundled against the early morning chill of autumn, Olive moved behind him and placed her head on his shoulder. They were exhausted. They had worked frantically through the night locating a boat, taking on board extra fuel and supplies, and installing a trolling motor for the shallow creeks.

None of that troubled Ben. His mouth was open, his thumb caught between his teeth, his eyes fixed on nothing, his ears barely hearing the slapping of the waves against the boat. He had hardly been able to process what he had been told by Miss Carly. They were words he could barely decipher as she pulled his head down to her level and whispered the secret in almost undecipherable gasps. It was something that defied reason. Then he had gone to see his mother.

Buck Tindal was worn out as well. The events of the day had closed in on him like the concussion he had experienced on a field in France. He wasn't thinking straight and that was dangerous for Buck. After Ben had rejected everyone's plea to accept Luther's challenge to rescue Rachel, Buck pulled Black James aside.

Okay, goddamn it, I'll do it. I'm going after her. I don't want to press you James, but I have to ask. You want to go?"

James didn't hesitate. "If it's Miss Rachel, I'm going," he said.

An hour later they were meeting with Jack Humphrey, an old friend who was now a vice president for the Coastal and Piedmont Railroad. Part of Jack's oversight was the records department where all the routes and locations of the tracks were detailed in maps neatly rolled and resting in bins marked by their coordinates.

"Here it is, Buck," Jack said, spreading a map on the table. "You picked a hell of a route to get there. Guess it's the only way, though, since you can't go by the river without being seen."

Jack Humphrey pointed to the legend for tracks on the other side of the Cape Fear River. They had been abandoned when the government confiscated the property to build a munitions depot during WWII.

"I've known you a long time, Buck, and I've seen you do some crazy things to catch criminals, but this takes the cake. Anyway, here's the way I see it. We've got this relic of a Railroad Push Car, you know, the kind they had around the turn of the century, two guys pumping this see-saw type handle up and down and each stroke moves the flat-bed along. Well, if we can get permission from Colonel Grandle to let us transport it through the munitions depot and out the other side, and if the tracks are still in relatively good shape, and if you don't get blown away by the weather that's moving in, and a couple of other qualifiers like Luther doesn't set an ambush; then you got about fifteen miles to go before you get to the switching station if its still there and if the parts haven't been, uh, stolen, and everything works after all this time, then you switch yourself off for another five miles, and, when you get there, if you still got the strength to walk another mile, well then, Buck, you're *finally there.*"

Buck knocked softly on Becky Porter's door. When there was no answer, he let himself in with a key she had given him—the one she said he could use in the event of an emergency. She probably was upstairs caring for Sarah. It didn't matter. With Luther's rampage and everything else that had happened that day, all he wanted to do was let Becky know that he and James were going after Rachel and try to catch an hour's sleep before he had to leave to meet Jack Humphrey and James. When he lay down on the living room sofa with his Colt .45 resting on his stomach, he immediately fell asleep and he was once again charging through machine gun fire and shrapnel when a hand gently shook him. His hand tightened on the grip of the pistol.

"It's OK, Buck," Becky said, laying her hand on his wrist. "I was hoping you would stop by, but I didn't hear you knock or come in. I've had so much to do trying to keep Sarah calm and the medications don't help much. She just keeps crying when she's awake or groaning when she's asleep.

Buck straightened his eye patch and ran his hand through his hair. He hardly remembered where he was and he had to stop and think for a moment. "Well, I came by to tell you I'm going after Rachel, and James is going too," he said. "Jack Humphrey at the Railroad got us a way through the munitions depot so we can take the back way to the hunt camp and try to sneak up on Luther."

Becky sat, and pulled Buck down beside her.

"Buck, I've got something to tell you. Ben was here a little while ago. He's changed his mind. He's going after Rachel! He and Olive are getting ready to leave as soon as it gets light enough. And I've got something else to tell you."

Becky began to tremble. Tears appeared in her eyes as she

began to speak. "I know of no other way to say it," she said. "Ben is your son, Buck. Yours and mine."

Buck Tindal swiveled and gave Becky a withering stare.

"What are you telling me, woman?" he barked, the shock making him sound as if he were a platoon sergeant yelling in the face of a new recruit.

Her voice turned into that of a small child. She started to cry and clutched Buck's arm. "That Ben is your son. Oh Buck, please don't be angry at me. I got pregnant that day in Raleigh before you were sent to France. I was so frightened. I couldn't tell my parents then, and when I went to the Army base in Raleigh, all they would tell me is that you'd shipped out. I kept writing and when I didn't hear anything, I almost went crazy with worry. I found out through my roommate that one of her friends who cleaned the Dean's office peaked into Mrs. Carter's desk drawer and found some of our letters she had intercepted. That's when I knew my secret wasn't going to last. I started to panic, and by the time I began to show Mrs. Carter had already told my parents.

"Well, when my parents found out I was pregnant they threw a fit, but when everything got under control, it was agreed I would drop out of school and go to this home for unmarried pregnant girls. And that's where I had Ben."

"God, Becky," Buck said. Becky managed a weak smile.

"I was living in a small cottage with three other girls and our babies when I met a returning veteran at a trolley stop. His name was David Porter and he was real polite the way people from small country towns can be. He told me his family owned a farm down state and he was there to enroll in college. Then he asked me about myself. I told him where I was living, and, well I had Ben on my lap so I guess he figured things out. We were talking when the trolley started to pull up, and he just blurted out that he would like to take me out sometime, and would I like to go. Buck, I had been isolated with the other girls and our babies for so long and he looked so lonely that I ended up going out with him. After a while, I could see he was falling for me and I tried to discourage it. Not breaking it off right then was one of the biggest mistakes I've ever made. I mean, I think we were just two of those people who had a need to rescue each other. That's what people with co-dependency do, don't they, try to save lost souls like we were at the time? David and I were so different in our backgrounds that getting married didn't make any sense. But its funny how you can deceive yourself, because it made perfect sense at the time and that's what we did, got married."

Buck put his hand on Becky's arm to stop her from talking. He finally had all but the last piece of the puzzle. "You don't have to tell me anymore about that Becky," Buck said. "The only thing left for me to know is why you haven't told me about Ben until now."

Becky's face took on a questioning look.

"That's the strange part, Buck, and I still haven't quite figured it out. When you finally came back to Hanover, I could see you had changed. I'm not talking about the terrible wounds you suffered. You just weren't the same boy I watched go off to war. Something other than your wounds had changed you, and I knew I would have to get to know you all over again. And besides, you had your hands full straightening out the Sheriff's Department after your dad died; and I almost never saw you in those early years. When I did you seemed so distant. I don't know Buck. I kept wanting to tell you but after a while with everyone looking at me as a struggling single mom with a mentally ill sister and troubled nephew, I couldn't drop the image."

Becky allowed herself to smile. "When they started the knitting club, I practically forced you into joining and finally had you where I wanted you. That's when I came to love you all over again. Oh, Buck, I've been a damn fool, and just hope you can forgive me and we can pick it up from here."

Buck sat quietly weighing the words he would use to respond. When he finally spoke his voice was as soft and modulated as if he had just entered the altar space of a church. "Becky, I don't need to forgive you, but if you think I do then you need to forgive me first. Let's just put the past behind us and go forward together and see where it takes us, I want to see Ben before he leaves. Does… does he know about me?"

"Miss Carly was supposed to tell him if it looked like we wouldn't have the chance to do it together, so he already knew when you didn't show up and he came here. But Buck, we don't need to see Ben right now. He's turned himself around and taken charge. I tremble knowing that he's going against Luther, but he doesn't need an emotional scene at the dock to cloud his thinking. Hopefully, you can get to the hunt camp in time to help him."

Buck reached over and pulled Becky to him.

PENDER
CHANGES SIDES

L uther Quinn stood crying in the dim light of the trophy room among the heads of the slain animals mounted on the walls. It had been after midnight when they reached the maze of canals that led through the saw grass marsh to the hunting camp lodge. He carried the body of Lenore as he would a frail child. From the boat ramp up a steep incline a half-mile to the lodge, her dead weight finally got to be too much for even a person with his physical prowess. There weren't too many like Luther around, but he finally gave in and placed her over his right shoulder. That's what Luther was crying about. The indignity to his Momma as her torso had bounced around on his back. Of course he could have asked "The Ape" to help him, but nobody was going to touch his Momma except him, and besides, Pender was trying to deal with the almost hysterical Rachel.

Luther kept his Momma in the game cooler that night, but the generator that gave power to the property was sputtering and there was little gas left to run it. Lenore would soon be spending the night in the rapidly warming enclosure.

As soon as he opened the door to the cooler early the next morning, Luther got a good whiff of the scent of his Momma's deteriorating body, but nothing was going to deter him from the moment he had waited for so long.

After he had sent a final death message to Ben through Pender, Luther sponged Lenore off and straightened out her dress then carried her in the rocking chair where he could talk to her and sometimes kiss her cold stiff lips. He knew this was the last time they would be together before he had to bury her so spent the entire morning recalling childhood memories and the happy days they had spent together before the bad times had closed in on them. The voices were in his head again, as strong as they had ever been, and he thought he heard her answer, "Yes son, those were wonderful, wonderful years for us, weren't they. I had almost given up hope that we would ever be together again, but I should have known you would find a way."

The storm surprised Luther, coming on rapidly, blasting the lodge with its ferocity, throwing oversized pellets of hail against the structure as if they were bullets from a machinegun gone wild. Pender wouldn't go far in this mess, but somehow the little devil would get through to Ben. Then all Luther had to do was wait. Rachel was the bait.

When the hour had come to place his Momma back on the cot he moved into the cooler for her, Luther spoke to Lenore one last time.

"Momma, I hate to do it," he said, his voice breaking, tears filling his eyes, "but I've gotta say goodbye to you tomorrow. They'll be looking for me and I need to get a head start. I'll be thinking about you every day, and you don't have to worry none about me either. I got it all planned out. Figure I'll hideout somewhere down in South America, maybe Argentina, and keep myself out of trouble the way you always wanted me to do. Momma, I'm really sorry about all those years we couldn't be together. If we had it to do all over again, maybe we would have run away to where Cyrus couldn't find us and I wouldn't have had to kill him. I don't know. One thing I do know Momma, I'll never forget you, and you can count on that. Now I got to put you to bed, but I'll come get you in the morning, I promise."

Luther gently picked up Lenore and carried her past the silent generator to the door of the cooler.

Pender stood guard outside the door to the room where Rachel was being held. Luther had made him responsible for feeding her and checking on her regularly. "I'm leaving this little bitch up to you," he'd told Pender. "I don't care what you do to her as long as she can still yell when Ben and that Olive get close enough to hear. If she gets away, you're a dead man."

It was a small room with one overhead fan. It had one window, but Luther had made Pender board it up. There was a commode and a washbasin crammed into a small alcove. Since the generator had shut down, all Rachel had for light were three candles that threw small pools of light in the otherwise dark room. She had not left the room at any time. She was trapped and helpless.

Pender had taken to knocking before he entered. Now, when he heard her respond, he entered carrying a small tray with a bowl and glass of water on it.

"It's venison stew," he said. "I put some rice in it for you. That's all we've got left now that the generator broke down."

Rachel was sitting on the bed. Her face was drawn. She had been crying and her eyes were red and puffy. She was looking at the floor. She lifted her head and managed a weak smile.

"That's nice," she said in a barely audible voice.

Pender watched her eat. She was a pretty little thing with a nice figure beginning to form underneath the flimsy clothes she was wearing. He didn't care what Luther wanted him to do; he wasn't going to touch her. Old preacher Brown would have flayed him alive if he thought Pender ever harbored those kinds of thoughts about young girls. Even if the mere thought of it had reached the preacher's mind while he was giving one of his favorite sermons about the "sins of the flesh," Pender could see him stomping back and forth behind the podium of the First Primitive Testament Church shaking his worn bible in the air, almost in a state of apoplexy, and Mrs. Brown sitting there on the first row with her quivering knees drawn together, twisting her handkerchief around her fingers until they turned red. 'Course, Pender couldn't deal with the idea of having sex with a normal looking woman or with anyone other than a circus freak like the fat lady, and that's something he didn't want to try.

Rachel picked restlessly at her food while Pender sat. When she had finished, he crept over to her with his index finger extended over his lips. Pender had something to tell Rachel and he couldn't contain himself. One of Pender's little weaknesses was that he couldn't keep a secret to himself, specifically from normal looking people he wanted to impress, and especially from a pretty young girl. Somehow he thought it made his appearance less obvious in her eyes.

"I'll be gone for a while," he whispered in a conspiratorial manner. "Luther's sendin' *me* with a message to your parents. They're supposed to be in a boat on the way here. I'm headed out to catch up with them, tell 'em how to find this place. Maybe I'll throw in with 'em to help you get out of here if they'll let me."

Rachel's face lifted. She looked straight at Pender. An expression of hope worked its way onto her face. Her hand touched his shoulder feeling the sinewy, hard cords of muscles and tendons.

"What about the storm? Where do you think they are now?" she asked, trying to control the excitement in her voice.

"Pulled up in some cove to get out of the weather if they've got any sense. But I'm goin' out the back way through the marsh. That's easier, and besides, the storm's got to blow itself out during the night. Don't worry. I'll find 'em before mornin' and make a plan to get you out of here if I can. Then, I'll be back."

"How . . . how are you going to do that Pender?" Rachel asked.

Thinking through complex schemes was not one of Pender's strong points. He'd always depended on someone else to think for him, and that unfortunately had gotten him to where he was now. But Pender was not stupid. He had heard Luther talking to the dead body of Lenore about his plans for escape. It was going to be all about Luther. He knew he was using Rachel as bait, and if he killed Ben, everyone remaining was dead too, including Pender.

196

"Luther's going to bury his Momma tomorrow," he said. "When he leaves, your parents should be here by then, and we can all make a run for it."

Rachel heard Luther walking down the hall near the room. The walls were thin and any sound she or Pender made would carry. She put her finger to her lips. When the footsteps faded, she moved so close to Pender they could hear each other breathing.

"What if Luther discovers we're gone before we get a good head start," she whispered.

"I don't like to think about it. For a big guy, he moves fast; but the way I see it, runnin' is the only chance we got. If we get out I got a chance to get straight with the law. Otherwise, Luther's never goin' to let me go free, and I'll go down with him when he gets caught. He's so crazy, you or me or nobody else don't stand a chance unless we all get away. Course, you got a choice to wait and see what happens. I'll even stay behind with you if you want."

Rachel gave Pender an incredulous stare. "Are you kidding," she whispered. "Let's get out of here."

CROSSING
INTO DANGER

Ben and Olive looked back at the floating dock one last time. It was empty. No one had come.

"Looks like if he's been to see Mom, and she told him, he'd be here," Ben said

"Maybe he didn't go, and that's why," Olive said.

"I know, but I don't get it. She had a chance to tell both of us before everything happened, and passed it up.

"But you weren't ready to be told, Ben!"

"I know. I can see that now," Ben said, "but it was looking at Miss Carly lying there on the ground begging me to take the knife that made me realize it. That's a sight I'll never forget, I mean her body jerking the way it was. Tearing at her clothes. Eating dirt. She was killing herself for Rachel and you and me. That's when I knew I had to go after Luther. Look, unless I get inside his reach and hit a vital organ, no knife's gonna stop him. But I got something that will. My Army issue .45. I still got it. It'll take Luther out with one shot. He'll think he was hit by a train."

By noon the sky had turned dark. Lightning illuminated the eastern sky followed by a rolling drumbeat of thunder. The wind blew foam from the rising waves like flocks of wool. Ben knew storms could rise quickly with deadly results in this part of the country, especially on water, and turned the bow toward shore, attempting to find a landing before the approaching rain obliterated everything from sight.

Ben spotted a ragged tear in the shoreline where erosion that knew a beginning but no end had toppled a tree of enormous age and root structure. The tree formed a jetty where it lay in the water. 'Ole Man River' would take it away in time, but for now it presented a haven from the wicked approaching storm.

Ben powered the boat until it grounded in the ragged cavity left by the tree's roots and raised the outboard. He climbed over the bow, dragging the anchor, chain, and rode with him until he reached level ground and wrapped the chain and anchor around a pine tree. Olive pulled a canvas tarp from storage and Ben dragged it onto high ground draped it over pine saplings in a grove of trees. Together, they secured the canvas with ropes tied to grommets, then waited for the storm to strike its first blow.

"I thought Luther was supposed to give us directions for a landing up river," Olive said as she huddled close to Ben under the covering.

"He told mom he would leave some kind of sign, but maybe we left earlier than he figured, and now the storm. He doesn't know where we are and we don't know where he's hiding Rachel. Time's running out. Tomorrow's the last day we've got to find her. As soon as the storm lets up a little we're gonna push on.

But the storm didn't let up. It blew all during the afternoon and night. Then the temperature dropped and the rain turned to hail. Ben pulled P-Coats and sleeping bags out of the forward hold, then went back for a lantern, camp stove, coffee, and K-rations.

Despite the weather conditions, Ben felt threatened, and insisted on standing watch first. Olive would go next, and then he would take the graveyard shift. She was nervous and wanted to talk, but fatigue and tension took their toll and she fell asleep. Toward morning Ben began to nod himself, and remembered . . .

. . . remembered her from that first night on the pier when Miss Carly had dived for the brooch. Remembered her as she grew

200

up in Dry Pond's black shantytown. Remembered that there had been something wild in those dark eyes and, when she laughed, the flashing of her teeth had excited him.

It had always been apparent to Becky and Miss Carly that Ben and Olive had special feelings for each other, feelings that went much deeper than friendship. Ben, looking at Olive's body in a thin revealing dress, sometimes thought it was something else, as well. As it was, it fell to Olive to maintain the delicate balance in their relationship between caring and passion. And that was the way the years passed until one day almost thirteen years ago when Ben came home from flight school with his wings and orders to fly B-17s out of England.

It was a Friday afternoon in the early fall. The residents of Dry Pond had banished the memories of a torrid summer, and already the smell of hickory and oak was in the air. Miss Carly and Olive were sitting on the porch when Ben drove up. He was dressed in his khaki uniform with the pilot wings on his chest.

"Good afternoon Miss Carly, Olive," Ben said.

"Look at that boy!" Miss Carly said.

"Ben, Oh Ben! It's so good to see you" Olive said, and ran down the stairs and stood before him, completely forgetting to call him 'white boy.'

At 5'10' she was as tall as he was, and her eyes were locked directly on a straight line with his. They were full of something Ben thought he recognized.

"Is it really true you're a bomber pilot?" she asked.

"Co-pilot right now until I get some combat experience," he said.

"God, Ben! I can't decide if I'm more proud or terrified," she said, and kissed him hard on the mouth.

He held her against him for a moment. "Terrified?"

"Of you're going to war."

Miss Carly's instincts, honed from years of exposure to the unknown and unpredictable, flared at the contact between Ben and Olive. As Ben approached the porch she composed herself and extended her arms.

"Let's sit down, and I'll fix us something to drink," she said.

The next morning Ben arrived with a plan.

"Olive, I want to see the river before I go. Want to go?"

"Sure, let me tell Momma."

Olive returned with a curious expression fixed on her face

"Anything wrong?" Ben asked.

"Gee, I don't know," Olive said. "She acted sort of funny. When I asked her if something was wrong, she just said 'you two be careful' and turned away."

Olive and Ben walked down a path that took them to a ravine that led to the river.

"I used to be able to walk to the river easily from here," Ben said. "What happened?"

"Must have been erosion from the last couple of hurricanes," Olive said. "Let's go to the right. There used to be concrete steps over there."

"Yeah, but look up at that platform somebody's already built for us," Ben said, and pointed to a tree overlooking the river. "Want to give it a try?"

"It's so far up. Think its safe?" Olive said.

"Olive, it's no big deal. In a couple of weeks, the Germans will be trying to kill me."

They stood beside the tree, looking at the rickety wooden steps that snaked their way up and up until they seemed to enter the clouds themselves.

Olive looked at Ben with a grin.

"O.K., white boy," she said, "but you ain't gonna look up my dress. You go first."

The platform was built between the main trunk and a large

limb at the top of the tree. Ben stepped onto it and gave Olive his hand and pulled her up. The platform was narrow, and they sat side by side with their backs to the trunk. They could see boats plowing their way up and down the Cape Fear River and could look into the next county across the broad expanse of blue. Ben slid his arm around Olive's shoulders and pulled her to his side.

"Wouldn't want you to get dizzy and fall," he said.

"Yeah, yeah, I hear you talking," she said.

Ben could feel the pressure of her body against his. Olive was smiling as she turned to look at him, and he placed his hand behind her neck and drew her lips to his. He kissed her hard on the mouth. He slowly withdrew his lips and before she could recover, kissed her again.

"Hey, Ben," Olive said as she pushed away. "Maybe this isn't such a good idea."

"I've wanted to do it for a long time," he said, and drew her to him.

This time she kissed him back, and he could feel the warm fullness of her lips covering his, and he became aware of what was happening to him.

Olive pulled away again. "Ben this can't lead to anywhere but trouble," she said.

"I don't care. I could be dead in a month," he said and placed her hand on him.

Ben unfastened the fly of his khakis and pushed his clothing down to his knees. Olive looked at him and started shaking her head. "No, Ben, we can't. You know we can't."

"Yes, we can," he said, and began to undress her. Olive started to cry and tried to resist, but her hands could not hold him off. When she looked into Ben's eyes and saw his passion, she stopped struggling. He lifted her over his knees and placed her on top of him, and she helped him. Then Olive cried out and began to move with him.

It was a still day with no wind, but the tree shook and swayed.

Three months later at mail call he received a letter from Olive. She was carrying his child.

Ben had dozed off and awoke with a jerk. A noise different from the common night music had awakened him—a twig breaking, a creaking sound in the grayness before first light. He rolled to his side and placed his hand over Olive's mouth. She opened her eyes like an animal suddenly spooked from sleep, and sat up. The sounds of early morning on the river were wrapped around them: the honking of geese preparing to leave to winter in locations etched only in their instincts, the last night sounds of bullfrogs and whip-poorwills, and the waking sounds of the creatures that lived in the marsh.

Ben and Olive sat frozen as if they were ice carvings waiting for the warmth of sunlight to release them. As the grayness that precedes the break of dawn gave way to the early light, Ben reached for his .45 and crawled from the lean-to. He made a 360-degree pivot but spotted no movement and made his way down the incline towards the boat. The tide was coming in and the boat was floating. Ben placed the pistol on the ground and reached for the line that led to the boat and began to pull the craft towards him. He glanced to the rear to see Olive emerging from the tent and begin to walk towards him.

Suddenly, a scream tore the morning stillness. Without warning a creature had dropped from a tree behind Olive. It was short with long arms and thick hair covered most of its body. It had a protruding forehead, and from its flattened face glittered two crystal blue eyes. In a flash it had closed behind Olive and put a knife to her throat.

"I'm Pender," he said. "One move and she's dead."

FACE TO FACE

"One move and she's dead." Pender's cry penetrated the stillness of the morning like the caw of a crow alerting the world that he is awake. Ben looked at Olive. She stood silent, expressionless, frozen in place, a statue suddenly waiting to be unveiled.

Ben's eyes dropped to the ground to locate his .45. Like a tossed coin that falls into a crack that one cannot immediately find, he couldn't spot it, and turned to the scabbard that held the Bowie knife. His hand trembled as he edged it toward the hilt of the ten-inch polished blade.

"And if you hurt her, you're dead," he said in an unsteady voice.

Ben squinted in the early light to see Pender's expression, to judge his intent, but the dwarf-like man was hidden behind the larger frame of Olive. All he could see was the hairy arm holding the knife and the peek of an eye.

"So why are you here, Pender?" he said, a flutter remaining in his voice. "Luther sent you to test me? See if his note had me all shook up?"

Pender looked out from behind Olive, his brilliant blue eyes in stark contrast to her dark chocolate skin. It was hard for Pender to believe the delicate looking man standing unsteadily before him could drive Luther to all the violence and madness that had taken place. "Somethin' like that," Pender said in a raspy dwarf's imitation of a circus barker's voice. "He said to tell you that he's goin' to slice your belly and watch you try to hold your guts in while you die. Then he's goin' to cut you up in tiny pieces and feed you to the alligators."

Pender hesitated before he spoke again. He took a deep breath and blew it through pursed lips. The sound resembled that of a lighted fuse working its way toward a stick of dynamite. "Look mister," he said. "I ain't got no dog in this fight. I'm just a messenger who knows there's a monster waitin' for you at the other end. You ain't no match for Luther and neither is anybody else by hisself. You got to turn back now while you got the chance, and let the pros try to rescue your daughter, if they can; or, you and this woman here can work with me to get her loose. Otherwise, follow Luther's instructions and die somewhere in the swamp."

Ben shivered from the picture of utter destruction Pender was painting, but dropped his hand from the Bowie and managed a smile.

"Tell you what, Pender," Ben said. "Let Olive go, and tell me about Rachel and the rest of the message Luther sent. You're right. I got no bone to pick with you if Rachel's OK. If anything happens to her or you hurt Olive here, you're a dead man."

Olive looked at Ben as if he were an apparition. Was this the same guy who only two days ago refused to get involved? As nervous as he obviously was, was he beginning to show the same spirit she had seen and admired before the war? The way he was acting gave her courage. She slowly began to slip from Pender's grasp. Pender loosened his grip and let his knife drop to his side as he thought about his response.

"Last time I seen her she was ok," he said. "I been watchin' after her because I could see how scared she was. I done a lot of crazy things in my life, but hurtin' kids ain't one of them. Anyway, she didn't have nobody else to count on except me, so I slipped her some food. Luther, he's really crazy. Spends all his time in that room with his Momma. Got her propped up in a chair and keeps talkin' to her like she's still alive. But you can smell what's happenin' to her, and he's goin' to have to bury her soon 'cause the generator that runs the power is out of fuel. Only thing left on his mind right now is two things—spending time with his Momma and killin' you. If he get's you, your daughter's dead."

Ben moved slowly towards Pender, his hands open in a non-threatening gesture.

Pender raised his arm to hold him off. "I had a good life before I messed up and got sent to prison," he said. "You can't believe what those muscle men inside wanted to do to me. Luther, he saved me from them, but forced me to help him with the escape. I didn't know he was goin' to kill that guard or any of the rest of what happened. Onliest thing I want now is to go back to the circus and the life I grew up in. That's all I want. So I come up with a plan to get Rachel, that's her name, right, out of there safe. That's all you want? Right?"

"Right! Look, Pender. You know what's going to happen. Luther's going down. It's just a matter of time. I think everybody knows you've pretty much been forced into this. You can testify for the State and probably get off easy. Otherwise, they're going to think you were in on the plot from the beginning. Main thing is, getting Rachel out safe. So let's start with how we get to where he's hiding her and tell me your plan."

Ben kept moving until he came face to face with the little man. Pender stared up at him but held his ground. "You're headed for Devils Head Point, about fifteen miles up river," Pender said. "Then you got almost ten miles through the woods and swamp before you get to the old huntin' camp. Actually, there's a lot closer way through the canals that cut through the marsh, but he's sendin' you the long way around for a reason. You never know what's goin' on in Luther's mind.

Olive stepped over to stand beside Ben. Ben put his arm around her. "You know it's *our daughter*, right?" Ben said and waited for Pender's nod. "Okay, next question is, how are we going to get her out of there?"

"Tryin' to sneak up on him by goin' the short way is out. He can see you comin' up the canal from the house. He's got a rifle somebody left and he's a dead shot. Pick you off like you was in a shootin' gallery. Best way, I think, is to wait until he goes to bury his Momma. Then you can snatch her up and run like hell because he's gonna tear up the woods findin' you. And, like I say, mister, I seen him in action. You or nobody else I know stands a chance against him."

Ben reached out and touched Pender. He looked down into the beautiful blue eyes of the deformed little man. At that moment, Ben realized there was a way to save his daughter *and* Pender at the same time.

"Pender, think about this! *You* can save Rachel. Wait until Luther goes to bury Lenore and grab Rachel and run. Olive and I'll be waiting, and I've got the gun. And you, Pender, will get the credit for the rescue."

Pender's eyes narrowed. He began to blink rapidly. It was as if he were trying to fix the idea in his mind that he could actually escape Luther's domination. That he could have a life of his own again.

"OK, I see what you mean. You want *me* to rescue her. You want *me* to do it."

"You can do it Pender, better than me or the FBI, or anyone else. You can save our daughter, and you will be free at last."

That day, an unlikely relationship was forged between Pender Hicks, the ape-like man whose only wish was to rejoin the circus; and Ben Porter, the nightmare-tortured war veteran who would face the ghosts of his past as he attempted to save his daughter, and the black woman who loved him.

SIDETRACKED

Buck Tindal and Black James were in a fix. They had been sidetracked, as Buck put it, but in this case he meant that literally. They were sitting under the cover of a stand of pine trees growing parallel to a section of railroad tracks that had long been in disuse and were now littered with debris from the storm. They were huddled in their ponchos like a couple of duck hunters fighting the rain and bone chilling cold while waiting for the honks and the whistle of wings. It was going to be a miserable day, but at least dawn had come.

Buck and James had traveled at a snail's pace since the previous morning at six o'clock when they met Jack Humphrey and Colonel David Grandle at the gate to the munitions installation. After their identification had been processed, they had proceeded to the rear gate and waited for the flat bed truck carrying the push car to arrive. The truck had been late due to a flat tire, and the mechanics of transporting the push car to the tracks was such that it was noon before Buck and James got under way. By that time, they could see the storm rolling in, and when it hit it obliterated everything and soon they were being struck by debris carried by the wind and had to stop and take cover. That's where they were now, more than twelve hours later, when the storm finally blew itself out.

Buck rose from his sitting position against the longleaf pine, stretched, and walked out to the push car and stared down the track. He frowned, then grimaced, and started to rub his thigh.

There had been shrapnel imbedded deep within the muscle and he figured the doctors hadn't gotten it all. But that brought up other memories and he didn't want to go there. Buck continued to frown as he hobbled back to Black James who was standing and stretching.

"James, there's a pine tree lying across the tracks ahead of us. Good thing we loaded on that chain saw 'cause there's no way we can move it ourselves. I figure we still got another five or six miles to the switching station and then maybe another five or so after that. We've got to hump it if we're going to get there before Ben and Olive."

Getting the pine tree off the tracks was harder than Buck had thought, and they were interrupted every hundred yards or so to move other debris. It was almost noon before they arrived at the switching station. Black James jumped down and ran to the switch. After a few minutes he called to Buck. "Sheriff, this thing ain't budging. We got to hike the rest of the way."

Buck did not hesitate. A cursory look at the broken switch mechanism, and he was walking along the track leading to the hunting lodge like a bloodhound tracking the scent of an escaped criminal, Black James at his heels. They had covered half the distance to the lodge when the track came to a trestle spanning a creek and backwater swamp. Buck saw that the center of the trestle and track on the other side had been deliberately destroyed. The creek and adjacent swamp now stood like a moat barring access to an ancient fortress. Buck looked at Black James who had a tortured look on his face.

"James, it looks like we swim and wade from here on in, if we ever want to get there," Buck said. Buck looked at his watch. It was approaching one o'clock. Could he and James reach the lodge in time?

THE ESCAPE

Pender returned a few minutes after noon from his talk with Ben and Olive. He had brought the boat through the marsh with little difficulty, and ran from the boat ramp to the lodge where he found Luther with cut lengths of pine saplings and rope for lashing the pieces together

"Where the hell you been," Luther grunted. "I expected you back long before now. When they going to get here anyway?"

"You seen the weather," Pender said. "I came as fast as I could. It's goin' to take them a lot longer goin' through Devil's Head Point."

"Well, I'll tell you this. I ain't waiting any longer to bury Momma. I'm leaving you behind with the air horn. You see them coming up the trail, you sound it off. I'll be close by. Ain't no way they can get away from me in these woods."

Pender helped Luther build the travois. It looked like the kind the Indians used on the Plains to transport their gear and sometimes their old and wounded. Luther went inside the lodge and carried Lenore to the travois and strapped her to it. He was crying. Then he hitched the travois to himself and started to pull it. He carried a shovel in his right hand and a carved head marker in his left.

Pender waited five minutes after Luther disappeared into the woods to see if he'd either forgotten something or, the Lord forbid, suspected Pender of conniving with Ben and Olive, and was coming back. Then Pender went to rescue Rachel.

At that same time, Buck Tindal and Black James emerged from the creek and marshland onto dry land and began to walk and jog the last few miles to the lodge.

Rachel was standing beside her bed, which she had made up as if she were an overnight guest straightening things up before she left, when Pender entered the room. She appeared calm, but Pender could see the fear in her eyes.

"OK, he's gone," Pender said. "We've got to get out now." He took Rachel by the hand and with his ape-like strides and long, hairy arms, pulled her behind him like a ragamuffin doll. They ran from the hunt camp into the woods and along an almost hidden overgrown trail that was to be their route to the river and safety. They ran like frightened deer. When Rachel's breathing became labored, Pender slowed their cadence down to a slow jog but still kept moving.

"I know you're tired, but we got to keep goin'," Pender said. "If your parents see us they'll let us know. If we somehow missed them, we can't stop to look."

"But what could have happened?" Rachel gasped, "I'm worried."

"So am I 'cause we're going to need their help before it's all over. Maybe they pulled the boat into the wrong cove or just plain got lost. All I know is by now Luther's probably found us missin' and is tearin' up the trail tryin' to find us. So we got to keep movin'."

The trail separated the woods from the swamp. To the left, a dark forest fell away into inky blackness. To the right lay the swamp, its fetid water filled with the detritus of decaying plant matter and rotting animal life. Sometimes the trail led away from the swamp into the trees, then led back to the water's edge, always carrying them onward toward freedom.

They were almost halfway to the river when Rachel suddenly pulled up and bent over. Her breathing was ragged, coming in big gulps as she tried to suck air into her tortured lungs.

When Pender turned to look at her, he was seized by raw fear. Rachel had kept up with him most of the way, but she was only twelve years old. For the rest of the journey, they would be reduced to walking, and at their back a mad man was getting ever closer.

They walked for another hour and came to a curve where a large oak tree stood in the middle of the trail, which split on either side of it. It was a marker he had seen on another trip. It meant they were two-thirds of the way to the river. Maybe they would make it after all. Rachel had had a chance to rest. Pender was ready once again to pick up the pace. As they approached the trunk, a monster of a man emerged from behind the tree. In his right hand he held a polished hickory billy club he had taken from a deputy sheriff he murdered. He pounded it hard over and over again into his left hand.

"Hello, Pender. Hello, little Miss Rachel," Luther said derisively. "Thought you two might try something like this."

Rachel froze. Pender stepped forward and raised his prehensile like arms and leaped like a flying bat at Luther.

"Rachel," he shouted, "Run! Run for your life".

Rachel heard the crunching smack of the billy club and Pender's cry. She ran as hard and fast as a girl of twelve could run.

DUEL
IN THE SWAMP

S omething was wrong. Dead wrong! Ben had swung the boat into the current that forced its way around Devil Head's Point when he heard a bump near the bow. Probably just flotsam caught in the current. He had increased his speed to make headway and pointed the bow toward shore when the boat suddenly shuttered from a strike below the surface. Something big and hard was down there. He had to back off. He threw the boat in reverse and heard the grinding as the boat slowly moved off the underwater obstruction.

"This far out from shore, it has to be a sunken boat or maybe what's left of a construction project during the war." Ben said.

Ben listened. The bilge pump had suddenly kicked in. They were definitely taking on water.

"We got to get this thing to shore down there," he said, pointing to an area about a half-mile from the Point. The boat began the slow process of sinking. He pointed it toward the shore. "I don't think we're going to make it," Ben said tersely. "Probably going to have to swim for it." Ben, who knew a thing or two about desperate situations, began to throw the coolers and other heavy objects overboard. Olive helped. Ben pushed the throttle full forward trying to get the boat on plane, but it didn't work. Too much water. The boat moved sluggishly ahead. When water reached the gunnels, Ben and Olive slipped into the water. Olive was trying to swim with her head above water but was floundering. Fear was stamped on her face, her voice that of a frightened child.

"Ben, I'm not going to make it."

Ben knew how to rescue swimmers in distress. He had pulled several out of runouts near his motel at the beach. First rule was try keep them calm.

"Sure you are. Put your face in the water and turn your head to the side when you need air. Hold onto my belt with one hand and kick."

It was slow going as they made their way towards shore. When Ben felt bottom, he stood and pulled Olive to him. He was grinning as he hugged her.

"You look like a drowned rat," he said.

She shook water from her hair and ran her hands through it. She gave him a fake punch to the stomach.

"You don't look so good yourself, white boy."

Ben looked into the woods. To the right, the forest was thick. To the left, he could see daylight through the trees. He knew that was where the swamp began. They would have to hug the shoreline to reach the point and find the trail that led to the hunting lodge. As they made their way to the point they came to crevices worn into the rim of the shoreline that they had to skirt. Drainage from the swamp compounded everything. It was hard going, but they found the trail inland that lay between the swamp and the woods and immediately picked up their pace. Barring any more obstacles, they would be at the lodge in less than two hours.

Ben realized the fix they were in but didn't want to upset Olive anymore than she already was. Without a boat their escape by water was ended. Unless Luther had decided to give up the vendetta and run, they were going to have to face him. If they met Pender and Rachel on the trail as planned, Ben would hand the Bowie knife to Pender and he would use the .45. That would do it.

"Oh my God," Ben suddenly muttered to himself. The .45 was packed in one of the coolers that had gone overboard. All he had was the knife. Maybe Pender could help, but it was going to come down to a face-off between Luther and himself.

Ben and Olive had traveled less than a mile when the trail rose to a small summit. When they looked down, Olive cried out and grabbed Ben's arm. Luther stood at the bottom. He looked as if he could have been a giant woodcutter, stepping out of folklore except there was no mirth in his eyes or smile on his face. He held Rachel in front of him. Her mouth was taped and hands and feet tied. A knife was at her throat.

"You looking for somebody, cousin?" he teased.

Ben looked into Rachel's eyes. She was terrified. He turned to Olive. She was trembling uncontrollably. He turned back to Luther. Luther's face showed no emotion, but his eyes were red with hate.

Ben tried to steady his voice, but he could hear the panic in it when he spoke.

"You . . . You let her go, Luther," he said. "It's really me you want, isn't it?"

"I've waited a long time for this cousin," Luther said. You shoulda known better than to turn me in and take me away from my Momma. They didn't have no proof until you went and found it. Now it's my turn. You want this little nigger, you come and get her."

Olive tugged on Ben's arm.

"Th . . . th . . . gun," she stuttered. "Where's the gun?"

"Lost with the boat. It doesn't make any difference now," Ben said, turning to her. "I've got to take him on. You try to free Rachel and run toward the lodge. There should be a rifle there. Then keep running."

Buck Tindal and Black James had emerged from the swamp and headed for the lodge. Buck was winded and limping. Black James ran ahead and rushed into the lodge. He searched until he came to the trophy room. The mounted heads of animals looked ominously down at him. Buck had reached the lodge and the two finished the search, backing each other up. Finally, they stood together in the silence.

"Sheriff, ain't nobody here. They all be on the trail."

"If he hurts my son and granddaughter, he's a dead son-of-a-bitch."

With that spoken, the two tired men ran down the steps of the lodge toward the path leading to the river.

Ben stepped forward to face Luther. His legs trembled. He had trouble getting his breath. His hand shook as he drew the Bowie with the gold hilt. "OK, let her go and let's get on with it," he said.

With the ropes still binding her, Luther flung Rachel aside and shoved his knife back into its sheath. He withdrew the hickory billy-stick from his belt.

"I don't need no knife to take you on, Cuz. This here will do it," he said, pounding the billy-stick into his hand.

Luther swung the club side to side as he closed in on Ben. It made a whistling noise in the air. Ben began to circle to his right, away from the strike he knew would come. He held the Bowie knife extended in his right hand, his left outstretched to parry the incoming strike. Luther started to feint strikes with the club, trying to catch Ben off guard. Ben was talking to himself: "Got to get inside those big arms to have a chance."

Ben feinted with a thrust and leapt forward. Luther stepped back and brought the club down on Ben's arm with the precision of a professional boxer delivering a crippling blow to a vital organ of his opponent. Pain seared Ben's arm, shooting up his arm and into his body like an electric current. His arm immediately went numb. It fell to his side. He dropped the knife with the hilt of gold. Luther struck again. Ben cried out as the billy-stick smashed his collarbone. He went down on one knee. Luther stood on his tiptoes, the billy-stick lifted as high as his arms could raise it, getting the leverage to strike the fatal blow to Ben's skull.

Olive ran screaming towards Luther. She jumped on his back and wrapped her legs around his waist. Her fingernails tore at his face and eyes. Luther roared like a lion in pain as her nails found his right eye. He dropped the billy-stick and caught her arm. He broke her grip and wound up like a discus thrower preparing to release the discus and flung her into the air. Olive sailed with her arms flailing and hit the big tree. She fell limply to the ground, her neck canted at an odd angle. Ben picked up the knife and staggered to his feet. Luther had one hand over his ripped eye. Blood was pouring from his face. Ben ran to Rachel and cut the ropes binding her.

"Run, Rachel," he shouted. He turned and saw Luther reach for him. He ducked and backed toward the swamp. Rachel was still untangling herself from the rope. If Luther followed him, Rachel would have time to escape. Ben started to shout and wave his knife as he entered the water.

"What's the matter, Luther? You afraid of the water?" he taunted him. "Come on and try to catch me."

Ben kept backing, his eyes still on Rachel. But she wasn't running. She was kneeling beside Olive and sobbing uncontrollably.

Luther threw her a glance. It would be so easy to kill her as she knelt with her back to him, but Ben's words and gestures were getting to him.

Ben began to pound his fist over his heart.

"Come on killer. I'm waiting," he said.

Luther turned away from Rachel and charged into the swamp. "I've got you now boy," he growled.

Ben's feet were beginning to slide and sink into the muck created by years of decaying plant and animal life that the swamp had encroached on and consumed. He was losing his balance. Luther had already closed to within a few feet. Ben tried to strike with the knife, but Luther parried his thrust and knocked the knife from his hand. He seized Ben by the throat and shoved him to the swamp bottom. He was choking him and holding him down so he couldn't get air. Ben tore at Luther's hands, trying to break his grip, but it was like scratching a piece of steel. Ben's breath was being squeezed out of him, and he could feel the blackness creeping in and his lips beginning to open to accept the kind release to death. The water was now in his trachea and his life began to flash before him. He was twelve years old and his mother had lost her heirloom gold brooch on the lake bottom. Miss Carly had dived in after it. "I was down there giving out of air when I heard the Loa, the spirits, speak to me," she said. "I put my hand out and there it was." It was all blackness now. Ben was almost gone when by some death reflex he threw his hand out and dug it into the muck. His hand touched the gold hilt of the Bowie knife. It was the death reflex that jerked the knife upwards.

Luther screamed. He stood upright and grabbed his side. One hand still held fast to Ben's neck. Damned if he would let go. Blood gushed from Luther's wound, the knife stuck there with Ben's death grip still holding it. The water was turning red when there was a swirling in the midst of it. A pair of hooded eyes broke the surface, their non-blinking stare fixed on Luther. With a swish of its mighty tail the alligator struck at Luther's leg. Luther cried out, and letting go of Ben, struck the gator between its eyes. He rained down blows on it. With its powerful tail, the gator propelled itself away from Ben, carrying Luther with it into the deeper water of the swamp.

"Goddamn you," he shouted at the creature, and it flashed its tail one last time and Luther disappeared beneath the surface.

Ben was face down in the water, the knife still in his grip, when Rachel got to him.

"Daddy, Daddy," she shouted, and pulled at him, struggling to get him to shore. When he could rest without his head being under water, she pushed her fist below his sternum into his solar plexus, keeping up the rhythm as she pleaded with him.

"Please, Daddy, please."

With a heave, water finally gushed from Ben's mouth and he began to suck in air. He couldn't remember, but in his mind's eye, he saw Luther being dragged under the surface. Was it really all over? Were they really safe at last?"

"Daddy, Momma's dead," Rachel cried out.

Ben struggled to stand but fell. His started to crawl towards

Olive, his adrenaline carrying him. He lay down beside her. He bent over her. His tears fell on her face.

"Olive, Oh Olive," he said. "What a fool I've been."

He sat and pulled her head into his lap, and bent to kiss her for the last time. He was rocking her back and forth in his arms when he heard Rachel scream.

"Look, Daddy, look!"

Ben turned to look where she was pointing. His heart raced. His mouth dropped open. He felt faint. There before him, Luther was emerging from the swamp. A deeply ripped open leg was dragging. One wrist was missing its hand, just a bloody stump there instead. His body was covered with muck, his hair green with algae. He was a creature emerging from a lost lagoon, a demon from the river Styx.

"You didn't think no gator was going to stop me, did you Cuz?"

He continued to drag himself towards Ben, his remaining huge fist punching the air. Ben would have to fight him one last time!

As Ben rose his limbs shook. Fatigue permeated every inch and ounce of his body, but his eyes had narrowed and the flint of rage was in them. The knife with the hilt of gold was in his hands. He moved towards Luther. They stood facing each other. Luther was grinning.

"Gator can't kill me. Knife can't stop me. Now you're mine, Cuz, and you can't guess what I'm going to do to you before you die."

"You killed Olive, you bastard. I'm going to drive this knife into your rotten heart."

Ben began to circle Luther. Luther tried to pivot to face him, but his torn leg could not keep up.

"Come on you little coward. That's what you've always been. Face me like a man," he said.

Ben stopped and looked at him. "Luther, you're going down," he said, and walked directly towards him.

Luther swung at him, and Ben ducked and moved inside his

punch. Luther clamped his good hand on Ben's shoulder, and then wrapped his bloody arm around him, pulling him to his chest. Luther's good hand was now on Ben's throat tearing at his gullet as if he were a chef preparing a goose for roasting. Ben had the knife parallel to his chest to keep Luther from knocking it away as he had before. He tilted the blade forward, and with what was left of his strength drove it deep into Luther's chest. Luther staggered backwards, his good hand grasping the gold hilt of the knife. He tried to pull the blade from his body, but the knife would not budge. As he tried to dislodge it, the cap that was fitted to the top of the golden hilt fell off. With it fell the diamond encrusted many jeweled brooch that had been lost into the deep waters under a pier when Ben was twelve years old. Luther had been standing beside him when Carly, the Voodoo priestess, had jumped into the chilly water to retrieve it. Luther looked at Ben in disbelief before his eyes went blank.

"Momma, I'm coming home to you," he said as he fell. His huge body shook the ground. The diamonds in the brooch glittered against the damp ground.

Ben turned and walked to Rachel who stood beside Olive. She was on her toes, her hands balled into fists. He put his arms around her.

"Honey, it's OK now. It's all over," he said.

There was a noise along the trail. Men running. Shouts. Buck Tindal and Black James charged into the open, guns in hand. Buck had to stop to catch his breath. Black James reached Rachel first.

"James, where's Pender?" she cried out. "Luther hurt him bad. I heard it."

"We didn't see him, Miss Rachel," James said.

"Maybe Luther throw his body in the swamp. Gators eat him. Maybe he crawl off in the woods. We look for him going back."

Buck Tindal had stopped to look at Luther's body spread-eagled on the ground. He looked at Ben holding Rachel. His eyes filled with tears.

"Ben! Ben! Son!" he shouted "Rachel!

Ben looked up. For a moment the meaning of Buck's words did not penetrate the shock of the traumatic events that had just occured. Then he remembered the whispered words of Miss Carly as she lay dying with Buck's name on her lips.

"Dad, Dad," Ben cried out.

Then Buck went and wrapped his arms around them—a son and a grandaughter whom he had lost and finally found.

EPILOGUE

Rachel Porter sat at a desk mounted against the wall in her customized motor home. The thermometer was pushing 100-degrees outside and the unit trying to cool the interior of the Winnebago was faltering. In addition to the built-in furnishings, this model was adorned with an assortment of questionable items. Dolls of various dress and colors were attached to the walls and there was a necklace with polished wolf fangs hanging behind her desk. A deck of Tarot cards occupied a space at one corner of the table and a thurible for burning incense was on the other. You would think that Rachel Porter was back in Miss Carly's Voodoo room preparing for an exorcism or a dreaded reading of the Tarot cards. But no, she was cooling off with a tall iced drink containing mango and pineapple juice spiked with Puerto Rican rum and relaxing while smiling to herself at the reaction of some of the patients to the Voodoo paraphernalia. A few of the dolls had needles stuck in them which always enabled Rachel to start a conversation even with the most reticent of those who came for treatment. The big difference between Rachel and Miss Carly was that there were initials after the name—Rachel Porter, MD, was a graduate of Duke University Medical School. She had just seen her last patient of the day at a carnival on the outskirts of Shreveport, Louisiana—a fortuneteller with tattoos covering almost every inch of her body from the neck down. Rachel took long enough to teach her a few things about reading palms. The woman left shaking her head with eyes as wide as saucers.

Tomorrow morning before dawn, Rachel would be on her way to another town on the carnival circuit and would set up her traveling medical clinic for all who came voluntarily and some whom she would have to drag in. Like many doctors and nurses who donated their services, Rachel's were free of charge.

When she made the decision to take her medical practice into the dark under belly of the carnival world, Rachel knew it was because of the dwarf monkey-looking man named Pender Hicks. He had probably saved her life by throwing himself at Luther. She knew Pender had the mind of a child and couldn't defend himself against the charges leveled against him. She wanted to find and help him if he was still alive.

A feeling of helplessness stayed with her all through college and medical school. Pender had never shown up, and searchers concluded that Luther had stopped long enough to toss his smashed, limp, bloody body into the swamp where the alligators, no doubt, had eaten him. That explanation didn't sit well with Rachel. Luther had caught up with her pretty fast, and she didn't think he cared enough about Pender one way or the other to take the time to dispose of him. Anyway, the matter had weighed on her mind heavy enough over the years for her to finally go looking for him.

Her father, Benjamin Porter, whose actions had captured the imagination of the press more than twenty years ago when they compared his heroics to the story of David and Goliath, had gone on to study law at the University of Virginia, and had opened a practice in Hanover. With the help of his wife Sarah, they had compiled a listing of small fairs and carnivals throughout the state where Pender might have worked. Her granddaddy, Buck Tindal, had joined Ben and carried the search a step further by using his resources with the National Sheriff's Association. Even Black James had pitched in until he came down with crippling arthritis and was forced to retire to Miss Carly's old house where he sat in her room and rocked in her chair and thought he heard her voice. But for all their efforts, no leads to finding Pender Hicks had been uncovered.

In her second year of practice Rachel caught a break. Her efforts had come to the attention of a Federal Commission looking into human trafficking and child labor in the entertainment business. Would Rachel be willing to lend her efforts to the investigation and take her medical practice on the road to locations pinpointed by the probe? She responded by closing her practice in Hanover for six weeks to follow a route prepared for her by the Commission. It was agreed that her attention would always be given first to those who needed healing and finding abuse in the industry second. Also, the government could not take into custody someone in her treatment until after they had been released by her. She had everything she needed, but after three years still no Pender. But she couldn't give up the work. It became an obsession with her. Then the press caught on to it and Rachel became the "Carnival Doc." Six weeks on the road became eight when Rachel remembered her grandmother Carly's story of her own road to becoming a Mambo and a healer in the Voodoo faith. Carly's zeal for her mission of healing took control of Rachel. She had always thought she would just be a doctor in her hometown, but now that wish was gone.

The carnival in Shreveport was tame compared to some of the others. Rachel knew they had worked to clean up their act and would make certain it stayed that way. It was time to move on.

The next morning before dawn Rachel was up preparing to push the motor home on to the next stop in Jackson, MS when there came a rap at the door. Upon opening it she was stunned into silence. Before Rachel stood a wee creature dressed in jeans with the cuffs rolled up to accommodate his diminutive size and a blousy white shirt open at the neck to reveal a mass of coarse, matted hair. Beneath large, crystal blue eyes were the ragged scars of an ancient conflict. In one hand he carried a carpetbag for his clothing. He took a step forward, cherry-red-lips cracked into a tiny smile.

For a long moment the silence remained so profound that even the sounds of a carnival waking from night were suppressed. Rachel finally caught her breath and broke into a big grin.

Well, hullo, Pender," she said. "Going my way."

www.ingramcontent.com/pod-product-compliance
Lightning Source LLC
Chambersburg PA
CBHW020411180626
46812CB00003B/924